Where We Land

ALSO BY DARYL FARMER

Bicycling beyond the Divide: Two Journeys into the West

WHERE WE LAND

Stories

by

DARYL FARMER

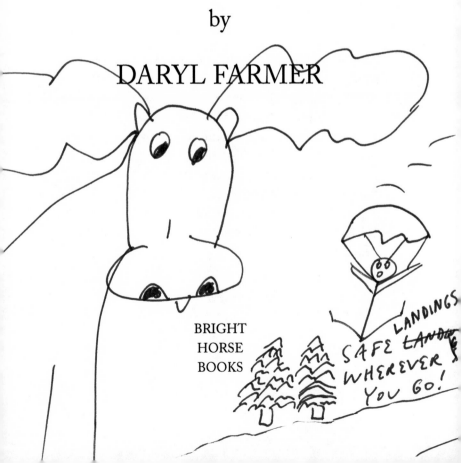

BRIGHT
HORSE
BOOKS

Brighthorse Books
13202 N River Drive
Omaha, NE 68112
brighthorsebooks.com

ISBN: 978-1-944467-00-5

These stories first appeared in slightly different form in the following publications: "Penance" in *Grist: The Journal for Writers* (online) 7, Spring 2014; "On the Old Denali Road," *The Fourth River* 5, Fall 2008; "Skinning Wolverines," *Hayden's Ferry Review* 43, Spring, 2008; "Glass Fragments on the Shoulder of Highway 375" was published as "Fragments" in *Quarter After Eight* 14, 2007; "Anniversary" as "The Chestnut Trees, The Wishing Well," *Gingerbread House* 12, April 29, 2015; "Flight," *Split Rock Review* 3, 2014; "Where We Land," *Whitefish Review* 13, Summer, 2013; and "In the Long Shadow of a Winter Morning," *South Dakota Review*, Spring 2006.

Cover Photo © AnthiaCumming
Author Photo: Todd Paris

TABLE OF CONTENTS

For Joan

Where We Land

Yukon

I DID NOT think of Garring as a dying town then, did not see the condemned buildings as a precursor to the future. It was the only place I'd ever lived, and I joined easily those who fancied us the proverbial quiet little town, a good place to be raised, far from the evils of the Denver and Colorado Springs crime that played on the nightly news. Yes, there was a prison nearby, and the railroad brought in occasional vagrants who lurked in shadows at the edge of town, and there was the standard small town drunkenness and fights, and longstanding feuds between families. At fourteen, I was not oblivious to any of this. Still, I could not have known when that summer began that my mother and I would leave in the fall, never to return. That I would smoke pot for the first time, something I swore I'd never do, or that I would have my first kiss beneath the oak trees that lined the schoolyard. That I would learn of the shame that had accompanied my birth. That Garring itself, at the end of that summer, would lead the city evening news, a single act of violence that to this day seems unthinkable. Over the years, the events of that summer have all run together in my mind, and I can't help but think of them as connected.

We spent the bulk of those summer days in the park at the end of our block. At least we called it a park, though it was just an old school yard with little more than a baseball backstop in a field of overgrown weeds and two basketball goals at opposite ends of a crumbling blacktop. The school itself had been closed two years prior, when it was deemed too dangerous to use and too expensive to repair. The building had been boarded up and pasted with "No Trespassing" signs while the school board waited for money they all knew would never be raised, and we were bussed to the newer buildings in Conway, ten miles east.

Despite the condemned schoolhouse, the playing fields remained, which was what mattered most as far as I was concerned. I had just finished 7th grade, and sports were my passion, especially basketball, and my daydreams filled with melodramatic versions of me defying great odds while leading my team to championships.

Most of our friends from school played baseball in the summer league in Conway. But my family only had one vehicle, an old Ford pickup, and Jack, my stepfather, used it to get back and forth from his job at the prison, or to run errands on the days he worked the night shift. I had no means of joining my friends, so we were forced to content ourselves playing one-on-one best-of-seven tournaments in every sport we knew. By "we" I mean Vincent Drysdale and me.

The Drysdales lived on our block, which was really the only block in town. Since I was a year older, logic might suggest I won the majority of our contests, but that was not always the case. For one thing, Vincent was big for his age. For another, he was a poor loser who felt nothing of resorting to violence when things didn't go his way. Once, in a tight situation during one of our baseball games, I hit a ball down the left field line. He called foul. After running the bases, I called fair. We argued. I pulled age rank. The next pitch, a full-strength fastball, caught me square on the jaw, knocking me to the dirt. I got up, bawling shamelessly for a thirteen-year-old, and walked home, Vincent right behind.

"What happened, Vincent?" asked my mother, glaring at him as she held a washcloth full of ice to my cheek.

"It was a foul ball," shrugged Vincent in a tone that suggested justice had been done. I pretty much gave him the close calls after that.

ADJACENT TO THE old school house and right behind the baseball field stood another condemned building, a building we referred to as "the theater" because it had once been used as a stage and band room. The building had strips of red paint falling down its sides, and most of the windows were broken. "No Trespassing" signs were staple-gunned to the doors, but that never stopped any of us from entering. The doors were locked, of course, but on the left side, behind the row of old oak trees, someone had busted the lock off a basement door. Inside rested old desks, a balance beam, sacks of old clothes and other props. Roosting pigeons fluttered their wings when we entered, cooing in mild protest before settling back into the beams. Dust made us sneeze, and the damp interior smelled of pigeon and bat dung. The previous Halloween, after trick-or-treating, we had crept inside. The town's only streetlight combined with blowing tree branches to create eerie shadows on the walls. The floorboards creaked, and bats swooped down from the rafters. The school year still felt new then, hopeful. Or maybe I just remember it that way.

ONE DAY THAT summer, Vincent and I were playing football when Ricky Dexter came strolling down the street. Ricky was a fifth-grader. He was wearing dirty Army camouflage pants and an orange Denver Bronco T-shirt. Ricky never wore a belt, and his pants were constantly falling below his waist, revealing the top of his butt crack. "Pull up your pants, Ricky" had become a steady refrain in our school, to which he would hitch them back up, and keep on his way. I remember him always with Copenhagen in his cheek, even in school. Ricky was the best source of beer in the county for kids under eighteen. His father's refrigerator was always full, and Mr. Dexter never seemed to notice anything missing, only that when he was running low, it was time to buy more.

The Dexters lived in a run-down two-story house two blocks north of the park. The house had been white once, but had long since faded into a pale gray. The floorboards of the porch were rotted, and there was a big hole where someone had stepped through one of them. The front door had no screen. One of the steps leading to it was broken and you had to take a big step up to get onto the porch. The lawn was full of junk, though you couldn't see it through the high grass. It was there, I knew, because I had mowed the lawn a few times the summer before, had mangled my blade on a broken ceramic coffee mug. In the high grass I found toys, tennis balls, rocks, magazines, even, once, a dead cat. The last time, my blade hit a broken bottle sending glass shards into my shin. I left the lawn half cut, and pushed my mower home as blood dripped down my leg. I never talked to the Dexters about it, I just never went back, never bothered to collect money for the half lawn I did mow. I was wondering who, if anyone, had cut it since, when Ricky walked up to us on the football field.

"Can I play?" he asked.

"Go away," said Vincent.

"We're in the middle of a game," I said. "Wait 'til we're done."

"I got some pot," he said. Vincent held the ball and looked at him.

"No you don't," said Vincent.

"Yes, I do," said Ricky and he pulled out the bag to prove it.

"Get lost with that, Ricky," I said looking around.

Vincent, though, walked over and tried to snatch the bag.

"Where'd you get it?" he asked.

"I'm not telling you," said Ricky.

"Stole it from your brother, huh? I'll tell him." Vincent lunged again for the bag. Ricky pulled it just out of his reach. Then Vincent grabbed him by the shirt.

"Let go," said Ricky. "C'mon." He looked up at Vincent. "I'll give you some."

Vincent let go of his shirt.

Ricky smiled, pulled a lighter from his pocket.

"Not here, you idiot. C'mon," said Vincent and started walking toward the theater.

"What are you doing?" I asked.

I wasn't really surprised, though. That the Duncan kids smoked weed was a secret to no one, and for the Dexters, it was expected. Stoned kids followed drunken parents, and I'd seen Mr. Dexter staggering around town, and had smelled alcohol on his breath when I'd collected money for mowing his lawn. Mrs. Dexter worked part-time at the grocery store in Conway. When I'd go in after school to buy candy, I tried to stay out of her line; she had a harsh rough voice, like a man's, crooked front teeth, and breath that reeked. Mornings, she would walk around the neighborhood in her house coat with a coffee mug in her hand. Jack would watch her from the kitchen window and laugh.

"You should make me coffee like that," he'd say. My mom would just shake her head and when I asked her what kind of coffee, she'd tell me to never mind and eat my breakfast.

There were two other kids in that family besides Ricky— Andrew, who was three or four years older than I, and an older sister, Marion. Andrew was surprisingly polite, a good student. "Amazing," people said about him, "given the rest of them." I never knew Marion. I asked Ricky about her once, but he just shrugged, said he hadn't seen her for a long time. Rumor had it she was in prison, or had been. Lawn mowing jobs notwithstanding, it was made clear to me the Dexters were people to stay away from.

As for Vincent's family, they had reputations of their own. Vincent himself told me he'd smoked with his brother, Duncan. So, it didn't surprise me really that he and Ricky were heading to the theater to smoke pot, didn't surprise me at all.

What surprised me was that I followed them.

WHEN THEY PASSED me the joint, I was sitting hippie-style, the way Peter Fonda and Dennis Hopper had in *Easy Rider*, a movie I watched with my stepfather on cable one night. It was an old movie. Jack just shook his head in disgust through the whole thing.

"Hollywood bastards make movies like this, then I gotta baby-sit their junkie followers," he'd said. "This is what I'm up against."

He seemed satisfied when Fonda and Hopper died at the end. But I was horrified. "See there," he'd said. "That's what happens." He looked at me and pointed. To him, the movie was a cautionary tale. For my part, I sat through the whole thing waiting for a plot. As often happened around the adult world, I was intrigued with what I didn't understand.

Now I held the joint to my lips and inhaled with my eyes closed. When I opened them I expected to see psychedelic colors, hallucinations—something. I was a drug user now. But, nothing. Then I heard footsteps, and turned to see the figure in the doorway.

"What are you kids doing?" It was Mr. Meyers, my neighbor.

MILLIONS OF KIDS all over America had smoked pot undetected for decades by then. I took one puff, and the authorities showed up. Vincent and Ricky jumped up and ran.

Mr. Meyers watched them, then looked at me and shook his head. "It's not like I don't know who they are," he said. I was still holding the joint. He pointed at it.

"Might want to put that out. You don't want to burn this place down, I guess. Come with me. I'll walk with you home."

"How did you know we were in there?" I asked as we turned down our street.

"I saw you go in there. I walked over because I was concerned with your safety. That old building's not safe. Then I smelled the dope."

"You knew what it was?" I asked, incredulous. Mr. Meyers was seventy-some years old, which was ancient to me then.

He laughed. "I worked in the high school for thirty years. I know the smell of marijuana, son."

"Never done it before," I said.

"Never busted a kid who has. Nope, it's always the first

time. Busted one kid three times. Each one was his first." He shook his head. I started to argue my case, but thought better of it. Why make waves. I liked Mr. Meyers. We were almost to his house, where I could take my scolding, and be on my way.

Only we didn't stop at his house.

"Uh, wasn't that your house?" I asked.

"Uh huh," he said.

"Where're we going?"

He stopped and looked at me. "You must understand, I gotta talk to your mother," he said.

I hadn't really thought to panic until then. To understand, you'd have to know my stepfather. That I would end up a crook was his single greatest fear in the world, and what he might do for my own damn good I did not want to imagine. Jack was never abusive, not really, but I feared him nevertheless.

MOM FEIGNED CALM until Mr. Meyers left, but I could tell she was seething. Then she dropped a bombshell that I never saw coming. Yet, how could I not have? All the signs had been there had I chosen to notice them. I had expected the usual diatribe: all that she sacrificed for the likes of me, the cooking and cleaning, the part-time job, and why? What good was any of it doing? Just as good to let me run wild for all the difference it made. I expected to hear how summer had made me lazy, the first step to mischief, and to be given a list of the chores that I would be doing from now on. Mostly, I expected to hear how much trouble I'd be in when my stepdad got home. I was fantasizing an escape, my new life as a hobo. A train ran through this town, and I was going to hop on. People did it all the time, I was sure.

But my mother just looked at me sadly. She looked for a long uncomfortable time, narrowed her eyes, pursed her lips, as if deciding something, and then I saw her tremble. Her lip quivered, and her eyes watered. "You poor stupid boy," she said, and then she slumped down into the kitchen table chair and wept. My mother, I know now, had been let down by men her whole life. I never thought I might be one of them. Of my own father, I knew very little.

"I'm sorry," I mumbled, unnerved by her reaction.

"Smoking pot with the Dexter kid. Of course you were smoking pot with the Dexter kid." She wiped the tears from her face and looked out the window. When she looked back, it was with utter disgust, and I felt the kitchen shrinking around me.

"Jack and I are separating, Aaron. So let me just say, your timing stinks." For the longest time I just sat, silent. But I disagreed that my timing was bad. I hate to admit it, but my first thought was how lucky I was to have smoked pot on the day my stepfather wasn't coming home.

I THOUGHT I was going to get off scot-free, but I was wrong. He may not have been there, but Jack was still the closest thing to a father I had. Mom called him at the prison that night, even though they had agreed not to talk for at least a week. I think she was glad for the excuse to call him. I could hear Jack's voice through the receiver.

"Where were you when this happened?" he bellowed at my mom, who, instead of yelling back, began to cry again.

It was one thing they had in common—they both tended to blame her for everything.

"Now I have a drug addict stepson. That's just great," I heard him say. I wasn't exactly addicted yet. I went to my room.

Mom came up later, knocked on my door. I was sitting on my bed, re-sorting my baseball cards.

"Yeah," I said, and she entered the room.

"He wants to ground you for life," she said.

"That seems excessive?" I said.

"We agreed to make it when you turn eighteen. Then you can do what you want."

I nodded. Honestly, that seemed reasonable to me at the time.

"Aaron, Aaron. Really? Ricky Dexter?"

"I don't know," I said.

"End of July," she said. "You should stop hanging around with Vincent, too." She stood in the doorway. I did not look at her. I felt tears, and hated myself for it. Then she turned and walked out of my room.

NEAR THE END of June, a new family moved into the house across from the school yard. Mom watched from the kitchen window, announcing each item they carried into the house, and imagining out loud what the furniture would look like once in place.

"They'll probably put that table in the back bedroom up-stairs," she'd say; or, "Ew. They'll never find curtains to match that upholstery."

When they were all done, she asked me to go with her and two of her apple pies to welcome them. I acted uninterested, but was glad to get out of the house, for the brief reprieve from my grounding. The family's last name was Watkins, and they were from Arkansas. The couple seemed old, too old for the kids that came with them—a nine-year-old girl named Alicia, and a boy, Rob, who was my age. As a whole, they were not an attractive family; if they were hoping for a town where they'd fit in, they'd found one. Alicia never stopped talking the whole time, and all the adults, Mom included, laughed at everything she said. Rob just rolled his eyes, though, and I thought he was okay.

"Any fishing around here?" he asked.

"There's Olney Lake," I said.

I didn't say anything else, didn't invite him to join me sometime. I knew I should try to be nicer, and hoped my mom wouldn't notice and lecture me about my manners later.

"They'll have to redo the wallpaper," was all she said, though, when we were finally out the door heading home, and I breathed a sigh of relief.

The next day, I heard the doorbell ring, and then my mother at the door.

"No, sorry, he can't come out now. He's been grounded. It will have to wait," she said. I went to the window, shocked that Vincent would have the nerve to show here, but it wasn't him; it was Rob, of course, with his fishing pole and tackle box. He walked down the empty sidewalk. I did want to go fishing, but I was relieved to have my grounding to save me. I'm that way still; when people reach out, I pull away.

IT WAS HARD to avoid Vincent once my grounding was over. It ended a week early. When I talked to Jack on the phone, he said that I was being "paroled for good behavior," but deep down I knew my mom was tired of having me around the house. There was only one park in town, and I couldn't really kick him out of it. So, against my mother's best wishes, our games continued. He'd been grounded, too, he said. As for Ricky, Vincent doubted Mr. Meyers had bothered to even talk to his parents. What would be the point?

The summer dragged on, the days grew hot, and our enthusiasm for sports began to wane. One day I was in the park shooting baskets alone when Mr. Meyers walked over.

"Any interest in making some money?" he asked. "I'm looking for help painting our house."

I stood, trying to think of a way to say no. "Ok," I said, at last.

He paid me ten dollars an hour, even for those hours we spent resting in the shade in chairs he'd made under an old oak in his backyard drinking lemonade. There were probably as many lemonade as painting hours. Every morning around 11:00 he'd ask Mrs. Meyers, "How hot is it?"

"Almost one hundred," she'd say.

"One hundred! Hell, I'm seventy-four years old, I can't work in this heat," he'd say, and then he'd look at me and nod. "I think this boy out here is thirsty."

"On the way," she'd say, and she'd bring a pitcher and two glasses on a tray, and we'd sit in the shade on the lawn under the big maple tree, where he'd ask me questions about my life and tell me stories about his own. He'd been in the Army during World War II, and had been in the Bataan Death March, held captive in a small cell for weeks with little to eat, and nothing but his thoughts to occupy him. I know better now, but it all seemed romantic to me then, like something out of a movie or a comic book.

"Every moment I spent in that cell, all I thought of was her," he told me, motioning toward the house. "I promised myself if I ever got out of there, I was gonna marry her and never let her go." I've never forgotten that. I am still searching for someone like that.

He also told me about his years as the high school janitor. It was a job he took pride in. It seemed he remembered every student that ever walked down those halls, including a lot of adults from town. He smiled when he talked about them, even the ones who caused the most trouble.

"Did you know my father?" I asked

He didn't answer at first. "He was smart, mature beyond his years, we thought." He paused, and I thought he was going to say more. Instead, he asked about my mom and Jack, and I told him that Jack was living in a trailer in Morton City, now. I looked at his face when I said this, expecting to see surprise, but he just nodded and told me it would all eventually be okay. I didn't know about that. Mom never seemed happy with Jack, but she sure wasn't happy without him. We sat in silence.

"He used to date our granddaughter, Marlene," he said after a while. "Your father. She's our youngest son's daughter."

I thought about this. "Did you like him? I mean, for her."

He smiled. "Well. They were pretty serious for awhile," he said. "We thought he was all right. But it didn't work out." He didn't say anything else. I searched for words to the questions I wanted to ask, but they would not form.

"Well, back to it, I suppose," he said at last, and I felt the scattered letters fall away.

We did not talk about my father again. We did not talk about the pot, that day in the theater. I never thought to ask him why he had shown interest in me, why he had been kind. Despite those long breaks, we did manage to eventually finish the job. On the day we stood back and looked at our finished product, it hit me that I would miss spending time with Mr. Meyers. After he paid me, I walked home slowly, counting the cracks in the sidewalk.

A COUPLE WEEKS after the Fourth of July, the Drysdales' station wagon turned onto our street, and I waved as it passed, expecting only Mrs. Drysdale, maybe Vincent, so I wasn't prepared for the blonde-haired girl who smiled back. Mrs. Drysdale parked, and I watched the girl get out of the car. She was wearing blue jean cut-offs, and a red and white striped shirt. Her legs were tan, and lean. I continued to watch, mowing back and forth over the same swipe of grass as she stood in the Drysdales' yard. She headed for her door, and just before she went inside, she turned and waved. I felt the blush on the back of my neck. I quickly finished mowing, went inside to get my basketball, and headed for the park. I'd been shooting for what seemed like hours when Vincent finally showed up.

"Who was that with your Mom?" I asked.

"That was Laura. You know Laura."

"That was Laura?" Vincent's cousin. I'd met her before, in summers past, when she'd come to visit, but I never paid much attention. It had been several years. Once, we had a water fight, and I had made her cry when I accidently hit her in the face with a water balloon. She had crooked teeth back then, and glasses. I tried to merge the memory of her then with the version I'd seen in the yard, and could not.

"What happened to her glasses?" I asked

"I don't know, contacts, I guess. What do you care?" he said, taking the ball from my arms and clanking a shot off the front of the rim.

"I don't care. Just curious."

I didn't bring it up again until we were finished. I beat him four games to one.

"Let's play again after supper tonight. Your cousin can come too if she wants." I tried to say this casually.

"Yeah, whatever," said Vincent, and he turned to go. He was angry that I'd beaten him

THEY SHOWED UP together later that evening. She had braces, and definitely contacts, because her eyes were aqua blue. I passed her the ball and she swished it from ten feet out.

Nice," I said.

"I play for our school team," she said.

"Aaron plays, too," said Vincent. "He's the best on the team." This was true, though our team wasn't very good.

We played twenty-one. Every time I got the ball I passed it to her. The few times I shot, I missed. "Best on your team, huh?" she said. So I blocked her shot. Meanwhile, Vincent was trying to beat us both. When she hit a fluke shot from the corner just over his outstretched hands to win the game, she threw up her hands in victory.

"Shit," he said, and grabbed the ball and flung it into the weeds of the baseball field. Laura laughed.

"You're such a crybaby, Vincent," she said, which was true, but he was a crybaby capable of violence. I stayed out of it.

"Let's play again," he said.

I started walking over to get the ball when I heard her running behind me, passing me, and I began running too, and passed her just before we got to the ball, and we both dove for it, giggling. I grabbed it first, but she tried to get it from me, and we were wrestling for it there on the ground, in the weeds of the baseball field, our young bodies touching, until I let her take it from me, and she jumped up and jogged back to the court. I sat up in the weeds, my heart pounding, a flush, dizzying sensation: something new, thrilling. I got up and jogged back to the basketball court.

All that week we played, every night until dark, sometimes past. We played H-O-R-S-E and twenty-one, always the three of us, unless we could coax some passerby to join us for a game of two-on-two. Vincent brought his boom box, and we would listen to the hits—to this day I can't hear Donna Lewis' "I Love You Always Forever" or the Fugees "Killing Me Softly" without thinking of her, of that summer—until the batteries would invariably begin to die and the music would fade to drone. When it rained one afternoon, we played soaking wet, happy for the reprieve from heat.

One evening, the sun casting an orange glow through the elms, the smell of fresh cut weeds, Laura showed up alone.

"Where's Vincent?" I asked.

"He went to Conway with my uncle." I passed her the ball, and looked around. It was unnerving being alone with her, and I felt awkward without Vincent there. We took turns shooting baskets without saying a word. Finally, she spoke.

"This is boring."

"Yeah," I said.

"What should we do?"

"I don't know."

"Let's walk over there," she said pointing.

So we walked to the baseball field and leaned against the backstop. I tried to think of smart things to say, tried to fill the awkward silences with words that would impress. But I was silent. We both were. We sat in the bleachers, and listened to the stillness, the hum of distant traffic, the birds.

"Do you like living here?" she asked finally.

"It's okay," I shrugged. "Kind of boring. I'd like it better if I could play baseball. Do you like it here? You must, you're here." I felt lame.

"I like coming here. It's quiet." She laughed. "I think mostly my mom likes me to come here. It gives her freedom to party and mate like an unencumbered adult. But she says it's for me." She rolled her eyes. "Because she thinks I'm stupid."

I let the words play in my mind. Unencumbered. Stupid. Freedom. Mate.

"C'mon," she said, and we walked again. I pretended to accidently brush my hand against her leg, and she took it, and we walked around the baseball field holding hands.

The oak tree grove at the edge of the field. It was dusk, that blue glow still in the sky. Beneath the tree, we stood facing each other, looking down at our shoes, or at the sky above us, avoiding each other's gaze. I was embarrassed at my clumsiness, and hoped she wouldn't feel my hand shaking in hers.

"Are you cold?" she asked.

"A little I guess," I said. This was ridiculous. It was nearly eighty degrees. I looked at her and realized that she was looking at me, too. I watched her close her eyes, and turn her head, and I did the same, leaning forward until our lips touched, and we kissed beneath that old oak tree behind the baseball field of the empty school house. I will forever remember it.

We kissed until she pulled away from me.

"What time is it?" she asked.

I looked at my watch. It was 10:30. "It's ten o'clock," I said.

"I have to go," she said.

"No you don't," I said.

She smiled. "I do and so do you." She was right, so, holding hands, we walked to the edge of the field, where we kissed goodbye and made our separate ways home.

I did not see her again that summer. She called the next day to tell me she was going home. She hadn't mentioned it, but that night was her last in Garring that summer. We agreed to call, to exchange letters, and for awhile we did. I watched from the kitchen window as the Drysdales' station wagon went by. I waved, but neither she nor Mrs. Drysdale saw, so I just watched until they turned the corner and were out of sight.

I would see her again, Laura, years later, in Colorado Springs, in a dance club that was all the rage. We drank beer together and laughed about that kiss years before. She told me she'd been scheming the whole thing since the moment she drove by and saw me shooting baskets. "It was just a matter of getting rid of Vincent," she laughed. We dated for a short time after that, a fling like many others that showed great promise before fading to stardust. I try to recall, did we ever talk then about Ricky, about her other cousin, Duncan? We must have, but I don't remember.

•

ONE DAY, A dog day, the school start looming, Vincent and I were sitting in the shade against the schoolhouse wall. We had been playing football, but after taking turns running for long touchdowns, we decided to quit. The summer was beginning to drag, and boredom hung over us in the midday heat.

Mr. Meyers turned the corner in his green Toyota, and I waved. I was hoping he hadn't seen us, because I wasn't supposed to be with Vincent, but he smiled and waved back.

"I hate that old asshole," said Vincent, as he picked up a rock and skimmed it across the ground. He had seemed angrier than usual, and I wondered if he knew about me and Laura, if it would be a thing that would bother him.

"Mr. Meyers? Why?" I asked.

"After what he did to us? What do you mean 'why'?"

"What did you expect him to do?"

"He's an asshole dickhead." He skimmed another rock, harder this time. We sat and let the words hang over us.

"My brother wrecked Mom's car last night," he said finally.

"Duncan? What happened?"

"Slammed into a telephone pole. My dad was so mad. He said he was kicking him out. He was yelling so loud. I didn't sleep much."

"What happened?" I was still thinking about the accident. "Was he drunk?"

"Drunk, stoned, high, whatever. That's Duncan." There was a long pause. "They both were."

"Both?" Who was in the car with him, I wondered.

"Yeah," said Vincent. "Duncan when he wrecked it and Dad when he hit him." He got up and started shooting baskets with the football. I watched him, not knowing what to say. Then I joined him on the court and we shot in silence.

We'd been shooting the football for awhile when I looked up and saw the familiar figure moving toward us, pulling up those camouflage pants. The day suddenly seemed very hot and I looked to the west. Storm clouds brewed over the distant Rockies. I should leave, I thought. But it was a summer day in a dying town, and there was really no place to go.

"Here, catch," said Vincent as he threw the ball hard at Ricky who had just reached the edge of the blacktop.

The ball hit Ricky hard in the chest and he watched it bounce away.

"That didn't hurt," he said as he rubbed his chest. His hair was in a mangled mess, and he had orange Kool-Aid on his upper lip. Looking at him made me tired.

"Hey, Ricky, your old man find a job yet?" Vincent asked. "Oh yeah," he continued, "I forgot, no one'll hire him, because he's a drunk."

"Yeah, well, he hired your mom last night," said Ricky.

"Take it back," said Vincent, moving toward Ricky.

"Yeah, and he'll probably hire her again tonight," said Ricky laughing harder then. I watched Vincent lunge, and I heard the thud as Ricky hit the ground with Vincent right on top of him. Vincent slammed him hard on the chest. That's it, I thought, it's over now.

But it wasn't over. Vincent hit him again, and kept hitting him. I stood and watched. I didn't move. I just stood there and watched.

Finally, Vincent got up and Ricky scrambled to his feet, enraged. Blood ran from his nose, down his chin.

"Asshole—fuckin' asshole!"

Vincent picked up a handful of gravel. "Oh yeah," he said as he started throwing pebbles at him. For the first time that day, he was laughing.

"Hey, knock it off." I knew before I turned, it was Rob. I had never seen him in the park before, though I'd seen him often working in his yard from my bedroom window. He seemed bigger than I remembered him from the time at his house and he was walking angrily toward Vincent.

"Can't you see he's bleeding? Does it make you tough picking on someone like him?" He shoved Vincent.

Vincent looked over at me, but I turned away. Ricky had a cut above his eye and a bloody nose. I felt light-headed.

"You better go home, Ricky," I said. I turned back to my shots.

"My dad's not the only one who's a drunk," said Ricky to Vincent, and when Vincent took a step toward him, Ricky turned and ran.

"You better hope you have someone to rescue you next time I see you, Dexter," hollered Vincent. Then he turned and looked at me, at Rob. I thought he was going to say something, but he just spit on the ground and walked away.

"I don't like bullies," said Rob. He wiped sweat from his face, looked at me. "Do you?"

The question felt like a challenge, and I didn't answer.

"Mind if I shoot with you?" he asked. I tossed him the football. He caught it, and looked at it as he spun it in his hands. I wanted him to ask the question I knew he was thinking. It is a question I have asked myself many times since then.

We took turns shooting, but only for a short while. "You can shoot all you want," I said, tossing him the football. "I have to go home." That evening, I found the ball, neatly placed on the grass beside our doorsteps.

We could not have known the future, of course. Still, I think of that day, wonder if a course was set in action. For years I have replayed it all, that summer, Laura, the Drysdales, Ricky. Ricky, blood on his shirt, Ricky running away. Who was that boy? I remember him in the schoolhouse hallway, tugging his pants, tobacco in his cheek, the bowl cut hair. One day, I walked by the junior high office, and Mr. Hensley, the principal, was lecturing Ricky, exhorting him to study harder, take his work more seriously, to behave. And there was Ricky, looking up, a light I can't explain surrounding him. I wonder what he was thinking, how his mind worked. He looked up, entranced by Mr. Hensley's words. There was no malice in Ricky; just an innocence that bordered on imbecilic. I envied him that sometimes. When Mr. Hensley was done scolding, Ricky, still looking up at him, asked, without any note of contrition for whatever had brought him to the office in the first place, "What's for lunch today?" Mr. Hensley, despite himself, chuckled, shook his head. Ricky smiled. The secretary, who'd been listening, smiled. Where would you be today, Ricky? I remember overhearing a man at the Junction Store just days after everything with Duncan.

"Shame," he said, shaking his head, "but probably just as well. The boy had no future. Such a waste of life."

I returned candy to the shelf, walked out of the store. I rode my bicycle home, pedaling furiously, not stopping at the intersection to look both ways, not even caring if I got hit.

·

MOM AND I drove to Colorado Springs and my Uncle Dan's the next weekend. I liked going to see him because he lived in an apartment that had a swimming pool, and there was a huge park nearby with two smooth concrete basketball courts, and a 7-11 around the corner. Mom wanted to move there, but I wasn't sure. I'd have to go to a much bigger school, and the idea intimidated me. Most of her family was there, and I knew I was the one thing keeping her in Garring. She wanted to move into the same apartment complex as Uncle Dan. I think she thought it would be good for me to be around him; later, this would turn out to be the case.

At that time, Uncle Dan was studying accounting at the university and he was an avid reader, his apartment always full of books. Just before we left at the end of that weekend he told me I could have one, just take my pick. I chose a big thick book, the complete short stories by Jack London. We had read *Call of the Wild* in my Language Arts class, which I'd enjoyed, and I liked the picture on the cover, a wolf, its head back, howling at the sky, with mountains and a setting sun in the background.

Later, on the drive home, I asked Mom about what Mr. Meyers had told me. About my father.

"Did you ever know Marlene Meyers?" I asked.

She looked at me. "Why would you ask me that?"

"Mr. Meyers told me she used to date my dad," I said.

"That was all a long time ago," she said. She sighed. "Marlene was a couple years older than me. She and your father were good together. Everyone thought they'd get married. They should have."

"What happened?" I asked.

She kept driving. She turned up the radio. I remember the song. "Birmingham," by Amanda Marshall. Something about second chances, an Alabama moon.

Suddenly, she pulled the car to the side of the road, put it in park, turned toward me.

"You," she said.

"What?" I didn't understand. I was fourteen.

"You asked me what happened. You happened," she said. I let it sink in. I did not look at her, would not look at her. She waited. Then she put the car in drive.

When we got home I went to my room and started reading the Jack London stories. They were about places far from Garring and Conway: San Francisco, Alaska, the Yukon Territory. I looked it up in our old atlas, found Northern Canada. It seemed to me then the most exotic place in the world. The people in the stories had great adventures, survived incredible hardships in the cold north. There were stories about wild animals and Eskimos. There was a story about a prospector fleeing the police. The stories became my refuge and I survived that summer imagining a winter far away. I would not learn until years later that London's mother committed suicide, that the man believed to be his father refused to acknowledge London as his son.

DUNCAN AND RICKY. On a Saturday, August 17, 1996, Jack came to pick me up, because for a short time after he split with my mother, he tried to spend an occasional weekend with me; I never really understood or appreciated him at the time, but as I think about it now, Jack felt some responsibility toward me, if not actual love. He did not abandon me, at least not at first, and he could have. I was not his son.

On our way back to his trailer, we stopped at the hardware store in Conway. I asked him if I could go across the street to the Dairy Frost for ice cream.

"Sure, kid," he said, and handed me a five dollar bill.

There was a high school girl named Angie who worked there. Every town has an Angie: the most popular girl in town, student council president, played volleyball, ran track. The previous fall she'd been the homecoming queen, even though only a junior. I liked Angie, because unlike most of the high school kids, she talked to me, and called me by name.

"Hey, Aaron," she said when I walked in. "What'll it be?"

"Vanilla cone?" I said.

She brought it to me covered with sprinkles, even though I hadn't asked for them. When I thanked her she smiled at me and I thought about Laura, that night, the warm breeze against my face, the scent of milkweed.

I sat at a table with my cone, trying not to watch Angie too obviously, when Duncan came in. Duncan was tall and thin, had bushy blonde hair. He always had tobacco in his teeth, and an old pop bottle that he used for a spittoon. He was wearing jeans, a brown T-shirt with bleach stains on the front, and a green John Deere baseball cap. I have replayed him in that moment a million times, searching my mind for some hint of what was to come later that night.

"Hey, twerp," he said, walking over to me. "I heard you were trying to hump on my cousin." He stood close, too close. He made a couple of pelvic thrusts, laughed. I could smell the wintergreen of his chew. I looked over at Angie. She was pretending to ignore us, but I knew she was listening. She picked up a rag and started wiping the clean counter.

"That's not true," I mumbled.

He raised his fists and feigned a punch. I flinched, tipping my cone, the ice cream falling to the table. "Don't worry, twerp," he said laughing, "we're all trying to get laid. It's normal. Ain't that right Angie?"

"Leave him alone, Duncan. Are you gonna' order something?"

"That depends. What are you gonna' give me?" he said, walking up to the counter.

"You're such a pig, Duncan." She was unfazed by him, and I envied her that.

I watched the ice cream melt on the table as I hurried to finish what was left of my cone. Then I headed for the door.

"Bye, Aaron," said Angie as I left, but I pretended not to hear. I felt shame for the mess I had left her to clean up.

WHEN WE RETURNED to Jack's trailer, I sat on his back step and watched the sun set. I closed my eyes and imagined that I was back in the Dairy Frost. I walk in just as Duncan, knife in hand, is about to rob Angie. He turns on me, but I'm too quick, and I jump on him, pry the knife from his fingers. I hit him, knock him to the floor, and hold him until the police arrive. Angie calls me her hero, and that fall at school, I lead the high school to state championships in three sports, the first eighth grader ever to do so. Angie and I go to homecoming together, after which we make out in the back of my new convertible...

Angie was perfectly fine without me, though. It was Ricky I should have worried about.

The papers said Duncan pulled the trigger approximately

two hours after I'd seen him at the Dairy Frost. No one will ever know why, I guess, or what a ten-year-old was doing out cruising with a seventeen-year-old and a gun, or if it was planned, or if Ricky just pissed him off, or if it really was just an accident like Duncan claimed.

SCHOOL STARTED SHORTLY after that. Everyone talked about the murder, the approaching trial. Rumors, opinions. Old man Dexter showed up at the Drysdale's one night in a state of boozy grief, gun in hand. The sheriff had come. Talked him out of anything foolish, I guess. Finally, about a week after classes started, an assembly was scheduled. For grief counseling.

The elementary assembly was first, and then we were called to the auditorium. We filed in, a little less chaos than when we usually gathered. As luck would have it, that day was the first Vincent showed up to school for the year. He'd been spending most of his days with his family in Pueblo and the pre-trial hearings. I had seen him briefly on the TV, walking into the courtroom with his family. Now, he came in with the rest of the seventh graders, walked to the top corner of the bleachers, sat down, didn't look around. I wondered if he'd known about the assembly before he got there that morning. I doubted it.

Behind me, a group of ninth-graders were joking about Ricky—talking about how he'd do anything to get out of school.

"Hey, Ricky," one of them said, mimicking Duncan, "you wanna' go back to school this fall? No? Well guess what? You won't have to," and then the kid pointed his finger like a gun and made shooting noises. His friends laughed. I looked around for a teacher to shut them up.

You should go sit with Vincent, I thought, but I didn't. No one else joined him either.

Both the high school and junior high school counselors, a handful of the teachers, and the principal, Mr. Hensley, a tall gangly guy with a large nose, each took their turn at the microphone. A woman I'd never seen before, a psychologist, said it was normal to be scared, to be sad.

After they all spoke, we were split into small groups, by grades and last names. Each group was assigned one of the counselors, or a teacher. The psychologist would roam around, so as to be available to all of us.

During the chaos that ensued as we moved to our groups, I watched Vincent walk out the side door. Mr. Jenkins, the P.E. teacher, saw him too, and turned, face angry at first, ready to tell him to get back in there. When he realized who it was, though, Mr. Jenkins just let him go.

I found my group. My classmates talked about Ricky, and other people they knew who had died. I listened for a while, but, eventually my mind wandered, and I thought about what my life would be like at the new school in Colorado Springs. I thought about Laura. Then I thought about the Yukon, about what it must be, trying to survive in that cold wilderness alone.

On the Old Denali Road

To NOT GET yourself in the situation in the first place: that was the key to winter survival in Alaska.

Yet, there he was. Walking into the wind, the snow stinging his unprotected face. On his head he wore a thin blue ski cap. His black Levi sheepskin jacket was not waterproof. The bunny boots he wore were warm to eighty below, but heavy and he felt their weight in his thighs with each step through the rapidly accumulating snow. He had decided to leave his snowshoes back at the site of the accident, thought they wouldn't be needed on the road, and would be burdensome to carry. He wished he had them now, though, in the ever-deepening snow.

It was late afternoon, and already the sun, wherever it lay hidden behind the gray darkening clouds, was going down. He walked in the tire tracks that he himself had made, less than an hour before. When he'd left two days earlier, he decided to take the old Jeep rather than either of their two newer cars: the Ford Ranger which he usually drove, or the Pathfinder which he left for his wife. He liked driving the Wagoneer, felt like a true Alaskan vehicle, had bought it on a lark from old Mr. Bagsby, the man at the end of their block. But the Wagoneer was lying on its side now, off the road.

"Son-bitchin' moose," he grumbled. He took a deep breath. Stay calm, he thought. Be smart, now.

•

HE HAD BEEN on his slow way home, from Fairbanks to Anchorage. A winter road trip, three days away from Nancy and their two children with an overnight stop in Talkeetna. He was a college professor, had been in the UAA education department for five years. In Fairbanks, there was a student teacher he supervised, and an inter-campus departmental meeting to attend. All of which took him less than half a day, leaving almost two whole days doing what he most loved: Alaska wilderness photography. He had been a skilled hobbyist since even before his professor days, had even tried his hand for awhile at being a professional, though he'd failed miserably. He could never quite make himself charge enough, and his equipment costs were always higher than his profits, had started chipping away at their credit cards. So he gave it up as a career, and maintained it only as a hobby. He was good at the photography part, though. His work was starting to be known. He had prints hanging in galleries and cafes, both in Anchorage and on the Kenai. He'd even done slide presentations at the Anchorage Museum of History and Art.

It was his way back into the wild, photography. It took him to the edge, alleviated his fears. Like the time at the Grand Canyon. He and Nancy had been married just a year. They'd arrived to the canyon after dark, and set up camp in the nearby National Forest. The next morning they rose before sunrise, and drove to a pull-out near the canyon's edge. There was no railing, just one small sign of caution. He'd set up his tripod, waited for the sun to rise. As the colors changed, he had inched nearer the edge. Nearer and nearer. Generally, he claimed to be afraid of heights, but he was focused on the world through his lens. He edged nearer.

"Be careful," Nancy had said, and he noticed a tightening of breath in her voice. He looked down, and realized that one leg of his tripod was setting precariously on the canyon's edge, four thousand feet of drop just inches away. He looked down and felt a tension, a queasiness in his gut. But it wasn't fear that he would fall, he realized then. It wasn't fear that he would jump, exactly, but he realized that the tension was caused by restraint. Death, he thought. Always there at the edge of things. A part of him wanted to know how it would feel to fall through that air. He looked back at her. She was watching him closely.

"It's why horses need reins," she'd said.

He'd had dreams since then, had probably had them before, of falling, of floating through endless space at high velocities. As a rule he was not a morning person, but he woke from those dreams alert, charged.

IT HAD COME from nowhere, that moose, came bounding on the gravel road in front of him, and he, driving faster than he should have, hit his brakes, felt the fishtail, spun to the opposite lane, and, trying to avoid a boulder, overcompensated, spinning a full 180 degrees to the other edge of the road. As if in slow motion he felt the shifting of gravity. The Wagoneer veered to the edge of the road. He could feel it sliding, tilting. He felt the drop, the vehicle around him slamming onto its side. Then, the silence of the winter afternoon as he reoriented. The sky was to his left, the southern mountains above him. Calm at first, and then the adrenaline came in a rush, and he felt his body start to shake. The characteristics of shock, he thought, but he couldn't remember. Pain shot through his left forearm. He tried to push away from his door and he hollered, a noise that came from the back of his throat, an animal noise that he scarcely recognized being of his own making. The arm was broken, he understood that then, and he pulled it into his body, grimacing, and he rolled onto his shoulder.

His head above his left eye felt wet, and as soon as he touched it he knew by the warmth it was blood. The car was still running. The cassette tape he'd been listening to had ended shortly before he saw the moose, but it was on continuous play. He was startled, then, by the burst of music. Verdi's *Rigoletto*. He listened to it briefly, before reaching up and turning the ignition off. He could smell gasoline.

He had to get out. No bad decisions, he thought. He had to be smart here. There were three ways. He could kick out the windshield, but it would be difficult to climb out without cutting himself on the glass, especially with only one good arm. He could stand and try to climb out the passenger side. The door was stuck, had been since he bought it. Would never open from the inside. But he could roll down the window. Still, he would have to pull himself out with only his right arm. A one-armed bar dip, and he at two hundred thirty pounds. You lard-ass, he thought. All the ways to die in Alaska in the winter. Avalanches, snow-machining accidents, hypothermia, plane wrecks, drowning. Driving your car into a ditch.

And there would be no sympathy for such stupidity. "What the hell was he doing driving on that road in those conditions anyway?" He could hear them, now, the rescue crew, sitting around their fires at night. Sick and damn tired of finding people dead. Smart, he thought. Be smart.

One year, the year after they'd moved here, a family of four had driven down this very road, when their car died. They'd tried to walk out. The night temperature had dropped to forty below. He'd often thought of them, walking in the cold night, trying to keep the children warm, trying to survive themselves. The family had all been found separately, two days later, by a search and rescue team, each frozen to death, the father just forty yards from an uninhabited cabin.

HE LOOKED AT his watch. Six-thirty. Nancy wouldn't be expecting a call until sometime after eight, after she'd put Abigail to bed, would be angry if he hadn't called by ten. Would not grow concerned until midnight. Had he left her the number of the hotel in Talkeetna? He couldn't remember. He thought of her and the kids, warm in the small house they had finally been able to afford. They had moved to Alaska in the toppered Ranger, Donnie just four years-old, Nancy three months pregnant with Abigail, their life's belongings—what they hadn't sold—in the small U-Haul. They'd slept in the back of the pickup, the three of them, for six straight nights as they slowly made their way up the Alcan Highway. It was late July, then, the daylight hours stretching to midnight, and he had felt he could drive forever. Donnie had been mostly bored by the long road hours, but perked up greatly at the wildlife they had seen on the way—the many caribou, the moose, and the lone grizzly bear cub playing on the highway in front of them.

The job at the university was everything he'd hoped it would be, and Alaska even better than he'd dreamed. After eight years of teaching junior high, a job he never felt comfortable with, and five years of grad school, at last he felt himself settling into a life of contentment. He was taking care of Nancy and the kids, rather than Nancy supporting him as she had done through grad school, and the university life suited him fine. The bills—student loans, credit cards—were starting to diminish. For Christmas, Nancy had bought him a used Hasselbach 6x7 camera that her father, who knew about such things, found in a California pawn shop.

After five years, not all of it easy—they'd been all but broke by the time they arrived in Anchorage—he would have to say now that he was happy. Settled, content.

But even in the most content of men, there is a yearning isn't there? A deep-seated desire for something wild. A cave to sleep in, an expedition to lead. Not to experience death, but to face it, to stand up to it. We hear the howling of the wolves at night and the hairs on our arms begin to rise.

HE'D SPENT MOST of the morning snowshoeing along the road that led into Denali National Park. He checked in at the ranger station, let them know of his plans.

"We don't recommend people going it alone," the ranger had warned him. She was young, broad-shouldered in her dark green uniform, had looked him in the eye when she spoke, quietly gauging his competence, his health. He assured her he was not going out for long.

The day had started partly cloudy, though Denali was hidden for good. The air had been crisp, clean. He loved the way the cold felt against his skin, the biting chill, his face tightening in the breeze. He had watched the late morning sun rise over the low mountains as he shot three rolls with the Hasselbach: of the snow-covered rocks on the riverbeds, the ice-covered trees against the blue sky, the light shining against the distant hills. A Stellar's Jay landed on a branch close to him, posing. Ahead of him, eight caribou had crossed the trail, though they weren't close enough for quality pictures. A ranger, not the woman he had talked to at the station earlier, a man probably his age, went by with a dog team, waving as he passed. He had captured the dog team rounding the bend, the dim sun a round light behind a translucent cloud, the lead dog with her tongue hanging out. Other than that, he had seen no one, and was glad for it. In the summer, he knew, the road that was now closed to auto traffic past the station would be teeming with busloads of people. They would come from Japan, Europe, the Lower 48, with high hopes of seeing Mt. Denali and grizzly bears. Many of them would go away never having seen either. Wilderness in a can, he thought. Package deals at unbelievable prices. On your own, you could do it for less than half.

That morning, the park had been all his. Alaska in the winter. Who in their right mind would do a vacation such as that? He imagined the question from his folks back in Oklahoma.

This time of year, though, the end of February, heading into March, was his favorite. The days were starting to get longer. The coming of spring was not felt in its warmth, but in its light. In two weeks, the Iditarod would begin, a sporting event unlike any other. Each year he would watch the start twice—the ceremonial start from downtown Anchorage and the actual start the next day from Willow. Donnie enjoyed it almost as much as he did, and Abigail, too. Last year, her eyes got big every time the dogs would pass, and she would shake her fists. "Mush, mush, mush, mush, mush," she would say.

Later in the month it would be spring break. The college and the public schools, for once, coordinated, and both had their breaks at the same time this year. He and Nancy had discussed staying at a lodge somewhere, where they could take a dog sled trip of their own, maybe even a winter camping trip, though deep down he knew that Nancy would never agree to have Abigail sleep in a tent in the winter.

He closed his eyes and stood in the silence.

Then he had packed up the Hasselbach and, ski poles in hand, slowly made his way back toward the station where he was parked. Overhead, the clouds were increasing. The wind had risen and faded like a sleeping man's breath.

Back at the parking lot, he loaded his equipment in the back of the Wagoneer, changed his snow pants for jeans and his boots for tennies, and then had gone to the station to let them know he was back.

"Made it, huh?" said the ranger.

"Were you worried?" he'd asked.

"Not really. Supposed to be a storm moving in this afternoon, though. You going back to Anchorage?"

"Naw, I'm just going to Talkeetna for tonight," he'd said.

"Probably a good idea," said the ranger. "I don't expect you'll have any trouble getting to there."

HE HAD DRIVEN to Cantwell, filled up with gas and ate a lunch of grilled cheese and tomato soup at the Lazy J Cafe. By the time he pulled back onto the highway, it was already starting to snow. He put a tape in the tape player, a collection of opera songs. When he'd come to the Denali Highway turn-off, without hesitating, he'd turned left. Don't do this, he thought. The smart thing would be to just head straight to the hotel, grab a beer with the locals in Talkeetna, relax and watch TV. The snow was falling harder now, and soon the roads would grow slick with ice. But he kept driving. He would drive, he decided, to the point where the road was closed. He knew this road was closed in the winter. A half hour, he had thought. Tops. Soon he would be losing daylight.

But then he came to a curve in the road. The snowflakes were falling like cotton, ticker-tape. Perfect, he'd thought. He had pre-visualized, since coming to Alaska, a scene just such as this, and he stopped the Jeep, got out and set up the tripod. In the next hour he shot another roll of film. When he climbed back in the car, the Jeep was covered with snow, and he had to scrape ice from the windows. He had to get back to the highway, he knew. He drove forward, looking for a place to turn around.

That's when he saw the moose.

THE BACK END, he knew. It was his best way. He pulled his legs to his chest and shifted them to his door, rolling, careful not to hit his broken arm. Slowly he stood, hunched over, and curled his way around the front seat. He leaned briefly against the back seat, and then pulled his way around it as well. He looked at the scattered pieces around him. His tripod was leaning against his side back window, which was broken, a spider web of cracks spreading outward. There were film canisters in the corners. The Hasselbach had fallen out of the unzipped bag, and had landed against the side door, the viewfinder in pieces, the lens dented. He could hear Nancy's voice. "You should zip that bag. One of these days it's going to fall out of there." Today, he thought. One of these days.

Once in the back, he pushed the top window open, stretching his arm as far as he could. On his third try, he got it to lock into place, to stay open. Then he pulled the latch and opened the bottom half as well. Gingerly he scooted to the edge and hopped to the snow-covered earth. His head throbbed. He tried to blink the pain away. Head injury. Don't sleep, he thought.

The snow was falling harder now. He reached back into the Jeep, stretching, pulling the items closer: boots, snow pants, fleece jacket, shell. He took the window scraper, and reached under the seat to pull his gloves and hat toward him. He did all of this with his right hand. He dressed, trying to use the vehicle to shield him from the freezing snow. He had no survival kit, that box load of gear that every Alaska vehicle should have in the winter: food, water, flares, hand and toe warmers, emergency blanket, flashlight. First-aid kit. Cell phone. The Wagoneer didn't even have a working cigarette lighter. He had a small box of camping gear, a butane stove, a Swiss Army knife. Cookware. A book of matches. He opened it. Two matches left. He imagined the voices again, the men around their fires. Stupid, he thought. Stupid, stupid, stupid. It was getting darker. He could feel the temperature dropping. He saw his reflection in the back window. The stream of blood from the cut above his eye was now frozen on his face.

A decision. A father found frozen forty yards from a cabin, he thought. Should've stayed close to the car maybe, been easier to find. No, no. Better to move. He had to stay awake, to stay warm. There were only three prayers, his father used to say. Please, sorry and thank-you. He lowered his head, put his hands together for effect. "Please," he whispered.

Then he started to walk.

THERE HAD BEEN, the previous summer, something else in that box of camping supplies. He remembered it now as he walked, the wet snow blowing into his face. An item peculiar to and sold at the campgrounds of the Pacific Northwest. It was round and flat and roughly twice the size of a hockey puck: tightly packed kindling, thickly covered with wax. "Fire starters," they called them. Just one would burn by itself for up to an hour. He had one, always carried it with the camping dishes, should have had it with him now.

Last summer, he and Nancy had gone backpacking with two other couples, friends from the university. Nancy's parents had been visiting, and they agreed to watch the kids for the two days. He'd been anxious for the reprieve from her parents, who he got along with fine, but for four weeks, all of them together, he had found more and more excuses to escape the house, university business that he just had to attend to. He wondered if he was fooling any of them. So he was thrilled with the idea of getting away with friends. They had kayaked out of Seward to a small island where they camped overnight.

He thinks now of that night. He had made the decision to use the fire starter, even though there was really no need for a fire, it hardly even got dark in the summertime. He remembers now, thinking consciously, better to save this for an emergency, probably. But he had romantic notions, the six of them standing around a campfire, talking, roasting hot dogs and marshmallows. As it turned out, the women had all three gone to bed early, and it was just the three men. Save it, something inside of him said, but he didn't, he burnt it.

He remembers their conversation now, the three of them around that fire. They had been drinking whiskey and telling stories, when the conversation turned to death.

"What do you think's the best way to die?" one of the men, Jim Wright, had asked.

"Plane wreck," said the other man, Dave Kimball, who was a licensed bush pilot. "One last mad quick rush, and then"—he slammed his fist into his hand—"it's all over."

"I'm never flying with you again," said Jim.

He remembers now, he had thought about it as he watched the fire starter burn. The best way to die. "Hypothermia," he had said.

"Really?" said Dave.

"Yep," he said. "You just lay down, and wait. When the shivering's over, you fall asleep. Very peaceful."

And then they had all stood, drinking, watching the fire.

THE SNOW WAS still falling. He could feel the weight of his boots, the snow growing deeper on the road beneath him. His legs burned with each step. It was darker now, almost night, the sky its darkest shade of blue, the trees by the sides of the road but outlines blurred by the blowing snow. His head still throbbed, and he tried to hold his left arm steady against his body. The wind was blowing needles into his face, his boots squeaking softly beneath him. He stopped. He felt his breath in his chest, coughed twice. He wiped his nose on his coat sleeve. He checked his watch. Only five. It felt later. How far to Cantwell? Seven miles, he guessed, maybe eight. But he wouldn't have to go that far. Where did the houses and cabins begin? He felt the weight of his shoulders, the droop of his eyelids. In his head a war raged behind his left eye. His eyes watered and froze, causing his vision to blur. He felt his heart pounding in his chest. Frozen to death: the words played in his mind. Don't sleep. Keep moving. Please. Sorry. Thank you.

He continued to walk.

DECISIONS. THE DECISION for fire in the summer. It was excess, always wanting more, the things you didn't need all that went beyond survival and comfort. What was once luxury is now necessity, his father used to say. A fire in the summer in Alaska, where neither heat nor light was needed. At what costs, the decisions made? The fire starter. If he had that now, would it be the difference between surviving or not? The question played at his mind.

He thought back to the moment he turned onto the road. *Don't do this.* Those were the words he had thought, an inner voice. A pilot had told him once. They had been up in the air, going from Anchorage to Nondalton in a Cessna. He was supervising two student teachers there, was going to check up. The day was overcast, but not threatening. To get to Nondalton required flying over the Cook Inlet and then through a pass in the Alaskan Range. As soon as they entered the pass, everything changed. He could hear the wind howling. The plane rocked violently in the wind, swaying from side to side. They entered a fog. Visibility dropped to zero. He had looked at the pilot's hands, tightly gripping the wheel and he stared ahead without blinking. I don't need to get there this bad, he had thought. At that precise moment, the pilot had made a

U-turn in the sky. By that time they were totally socked in. He wondered if the pilot knew where the mountains were. He had read of Cessnas flying into mountains. The pilot was sitting straight up in his seat.

He had closed his eyes.

When he opened them, maybe only ten minutes later, they were back over the Inlet. The pilot was slumped in his seat, casually eating from a bag of chips. When they landed back in Anchorage, they shared a cup of coffee, and he asked the pilot: Did you know where the mountains were?

The pilot didn't smile. "Not exactly a hundred percent sure," he said.

"How do you decide when to turn back?" he asked the pilot.

"There's a voice inside. Every pilot has one. The best of us learn to listen to it. I don't know if it's God, Zeus, some internal IQ I didn't know I had, some kind of instinct, but I never argue with that voice. Ever."

Don't do this. He heard it clearly when he turned onto the road. But he hadn't listened.

THE WIND GREW stronger. His glasses which he'd been wiping clean with his gloves became so smudged that they more impaired than improved his vision. He removed them, folded them clumsily, placed them in his inside jacket pocket. He squinted, blinking the blowing snow out of his eyes. The snow was growing deeper and he had to lift his boots higher with each step. He felt the burning in his legs, the stiffening pain in his arm. He removed his cap, and snow fell down the back of his neck. He shivered. He felt the numb warmth of exhaustion slowly overtaking him, enticing him to sleep. Odysseus'

Sirens, he thought. Keep moving. The throbbing in his head had decreased slightly. Don't sleep, he thought. Don't stop.

It was fully night, by then, but not entirely dark. He could make out the outlines of trees, the snow and clouds combining to cast a yellowish gray over the night. The willows stood frigid against the road side.

He came to the end of a soft rise, and when he looked over he could see the road leading into the distance through the forest.

His breathing was becoming increasingly labored. He felt his sweat beneath the layers of clothes. He stopped to rest, took several deep breaths. It was important not to sweat. He had to keep his body dry. He stood at the top of the rise and turned his back to the wind before him. When the urge to sit down became almost too much to resist, he turned and started down the rise. He moved slowly, each step like lead. One foot in front of the other, he thought. The little engine that could. Please. He cradled his left arm close to his body. When he moved it at all, even tried to turn his wrist, the pain shot through him, and the whole arm started to shake.

The wind diminished as he moved downward. The trees were higher here, closer to the road offering more protection. But he could feel the temperature dropping, the cold against his legs. His lips had grown numb. He held his right gloved hand to them trying to warm them as he walked. The air filled with the silence of falling snow, a silence broken only by the occasional snapping of a tree branch. His ears had grown colder as well, and started to ache.

Too late to turn back, he wondered? Get to the Jeep, try to spend the night inside. It would protect him from the snow, but not the cold. He put his right fingers to his temple and rubbed. He had to keep moving.

Widow, he thought. He tried to picture Nancy, tried to imagine the word applying to her. Single mother. He imagined Abigail, her little face, the blue eyes and pug nose peering out from her pink hooded fur-lined parka. And Donnie, with his short cropped brown hair, always eager to please, the two of them driving through Anchorage, looking for moose watching the planes take off over Point Woronzof.

Last weekend. He and Abigail and Donnie and the snowman they'd built in the backyard, teaching Abby to make angels in the snow, Nancy with the camera. He imagined the photo she had taken, he and the kids and the snowman, imagined it developed and in a frame on the mantle, always the image they would remember him by.

He might have cried, then, he couldn't be sure, his eyes already watering in the wind and the cold and the snow. He felt the throbbing in his head, his arm, the increasing pain coming from inside his ear. The voice of the sirens. Lie down. The best way to die, he had said, easy to say by the warmth of the fire. Just lie down and wait. Peaceful.

Dying is not an option. A line from a movie, he thought, which one he wasn't sure. He used it as a mantra. Not an option, he thought, not an option not an option as he made his way down to the bottom of the rise.

At the bottom of the hill was a narrow bridge. He took three steps onto the bridge and his feet slipped out from under him. Instinctively he put out his left arm to break his fall. He cried out at the pain, rolled over onto his right shoulder, holding the fractured limb close to his body, moaning as he lay on the ground. His face stung cold, his mouth full of snow. He crawled to the edge of the bridge and pulled himself up on the railing with his one good arm.

"Dammit," he hollered. He felt the rage run through him, imagined a wounded animal. He kicked the railing, kicked it again.

Calm, he thought, calm. Sorry, please, thank you. Not an option, he thought. Smart. Be smart. His cheeks burned, inside and out—from the cold, from the rage. He tried to wipe his face dry with his coat sleeve. He reached into his coat pocket and pulled out his glasses. They were broken, the glass cracked, the frames bent. He held them in his gloved right hand and made a tight fist around them, smashing them further. Then he threw them as far as he could into the woods. His head was pounding again, and he felt himself shiver. Keep moving, he thought. Keep moving. He used the bridge rail to guide himself across the icy bridge. Then he moved back onto the road, where the tire tracks were now nearly buried by the still-falling snow. He tried to take longer strides, tried to move faster, while still conserving his energy.

If he had the fire starter, he thought. If he at least had that.

How far? He looked at his watch. Nearly eight o'clock, now. He imagined Nancy, Abigail on her lap, Donnie playing by her feet, the three of them alone in the house. Keep moving. Not an option, death. One foot in front of the other. He felt his legs growing heavier with each step, his head lighter. The pain from his ears had extended into his teeth and jaw.

Death. Always there at the edge of things. Those were the edges he had played at. Walked right up to the boundary and tempted it, dared it to take him.

•

MEXICO. HE HAD been younger then, just out of college, spring break his first year teaching, single, free. He took a train into the country, and then ferried across the Gulf of California, camped on the beach, had brought nothing but a small pack of tortillas at a store in a nearby village. He carried a small bottle of water, a flask of tequila. In the late afternoon he woke from a nap to the sound of Spanish voices, all men. Fishermen—they had moored their boats and were up the beach. He approached them, bought some fish which he cooked over the fire and ate that night—one of the best meals he ever had.

That night the men came to him, asked him to join them. They drank tequila. One of the men had offered him a pill, he didn't even ask what it was.

The fish on his plate had come to life, wanted to swim. He'd run to the water's edge and flung his fish into the water. "Free," he hollered. "Go free." The Mexican fisherman had laughed. Then, he heard trumpets. He sang songs in broken Spanish, making up the words as he went, all to the amusement of the fishermen.

That night, late, maybe past midnight, one of the men asked him if he wanted to go out on the ocean. It was pitch black as they stepped into the small row boat, and headed out to sea. He was sober by then, for the most part, understood the stakes.

He thought about that night now as he walked, just he and the Mexican man whose name he never knew, the night so black he couldn't even see the bottom of the boat, couldn't see the man rowing in front of him, didn't know where they were, the rocking of the small boat and the lapping of the waves against its sides, the stars above, the rest pitch black, somewhere floating in the Gulf of California.

HIS LIPS WERE numb now; he no longer felt the cold. Each step was a stumble forward, his legs heavy, his eyelids drooping shut, the stinging of snow against his cheeks unnoticeable.

And his hands. He tried to move the fingers within his gloves. He could see his hands move, but could not feel them, could not will the fingers to move individually. The pain in his broken arm was a throbbing that had taken over his body, a steady rhythmic pounding that played inside his skull, nausea not only in his gut, but in his joints, his knees, his jaw. The pain, though, was gone, and mostly what he felt was numb. *Easy* he had said that summer. *Wait for the shivering to end, lie down. Go to sleep.*

The cabin. That man had died just yards from a cabin. There had to be places all along this road coming up soon. Keep moving, he thought, like a boxer, punch drunk and weary. One more round, he thought. One more round.

He continued to move, the snow still playing at his face, his hands and feet like lead as he walked. The cabin, he thought. Find a cabin, a break in the road. The snow still fell, steady, insistent. He could feel the freeze in his nostrils, his eyebrows.

He stumbled twice, the lead he'd felt with each step in his feet had spread, up his legs, to his thighs. He was all weight now. Dead weight. The word played in his mind. The weight was in his back too, and on his shoulders as he stooped in the cold.

He stopped. Waited for the weight to overtake him. Waited to fall right there on the edge of the road, where his body would be found shortly after his wife reported him missing. Frozen. Stiff. Already he felt his hands the precursor to the death he was sure to suffer.

He stood and closed his eyes, listened to the wind through the brush.

HE HEARD STILLNESS, the dying of the wind, a temporary break of calm. The road flattened, and spruce trees rose on each side of him. He opened his eyes. It was not black out, but a dark blue, the light reflected in the snow enough to see into the night. Without his glasses, it was blurry, but he saw it. A break in the road, off to the left, just yards ahead. A driveway perhaps. And then, behind the trees, standing like a mirage in the wilderness, he saw what he thought might be the edge of a rooftop.

Keep moving he thought, the sight of the small building invigorating him slightly. He stood, staggering to his feet. He took a small step, and then another. Not an option, he thought.

He stumbled slowly through the night. The snow, as if to dispute his last hope for survival, started to fall in a rush then, angrily, the wind coming in gusts as he inched forward.

At last, he came to the chained off driveway of the cabin. The snow in the driveway was deeper than on the road. He could neither lift his boots over the chain, nor bend down to crawl beneath it, so he walked around it, and then up onto the driveway where the snow was deeper, much deeper as the drive had probably not been plowed all winter.

He stepped onto the drive, and his leg sunk, up to just

above his knees. He took another step, then another, each time sinking into the deep snow. He stopped and looked at the cabin, the teasing cabin just ten to twenty yards, he thought, just that, and he imagined the man before him, standing just forty yards from the cabin, knowing perhaps that his family had already not survived. He understood then, the father had made a decision. He had heard the voice, had ignored it, had stood looking at that cabin. He could have saved himself perhaps, that man, but would have had to live forever with what had happened to his family.

He understood then, that the man had looked at that cabin forty yards away and had made the decision to sit down in the snow, had watched that cabin behind the blur of moist eyes, and then that man had lain down and waited. It was easy. There had been no other choice.

He took three deep breaths, and then plowed ahead, one foot in front of the other, moving the snow, pushing, moving forward, counting each step, one, two, his hands stuck in a permanent curl, his legs wet and frozen through his jeans, the throbbing of his heart, his beating heart, the crackling inside his ears as he swallowed, his broken arm at his side, he pushed forward counting, thirty, thirty one...

Thirty-seven steps, and he was at the door. With his boots, he cleared the snow that blocked the screen door, and then he opened it. He didn't know whether the door was locked or not, couldn't turn the knob anyway, so frozen were his hands, couldn't even maneuver the gloves off his frozen fingers. He put his right shoulder against the door, and then reared back, and slammed his shoulder into it. Tried it three times, but the door didn't budge.

He moved to the rear of the cabin, where there was a covered porch. He walked onto the porch. There was another door, much like the front. It too would not budge. He was panting now, put his hands on his knees, took several breaths. When he stood, he felt the stiffness in his back, the burn in his thighs. His heart pounded. Beside the door was a large window. He took his right forearm and smashed the window. Breaking glass shattered the night.

He lifted each leg over the sill, careful not to cut himself on the glass. Inside, the cabin was dark, smelled like old blankets, mildew. The wind blew makeshift white curtains around the broken window. He fell to his knees on the cabin floor. There was an old sofa, covered with quilts, and an afghan. He crawled to it, and pulled the blankets around him. His breathing was labored, heavy, until he felt it soften, felt his heartbeat slow to a steady rhythm, felt the warmth of his breath as he exhaled relief into the musty cabin air.

Hurdles

A SNOWY OCTOBER night, the air hovering cold in the valley. Dorm Halloween party, beer everywhere, people in absurd costumes. Damien is a sophomore and an undeclared major. He takes classes that look interesting at the time. And they are interesting! There's so much to learn! They tell him he will have to decide soon. "What do you like most?" his advisor recently asked him. "Electives," he answered and the advisor had frowned. Damien wants to please others, he does. But to decide once and for all the direction of your life. It is daunting, and what if he chooses wrong? Tonight, he will not think about that. Tonight, Damien wears a mask he bought on a whim at a thrift store, a bald-headed ogre with a wart on the chin, tufts of gray above the ears. Last weekend, he slept with a psych major named Roxanne. She is here now, at this very party, refusing to meet his eyes, in her fishnet gloves, staying somehow far away from him, in a slinky black dress. She's dyed her hair black. He likes it. It seems to enhance the secret they share, that night, which was beautiful, and he doesn't know why she doesn't dwell on the goodness of it. Damien first saw Roxanne in an art appreciation class, where, unbeknownst to her, he sketched her from across the lecture hall. He stores those sketches inside a book of Nan Goldin photographs he keeps on a low shelf beside his bed. The morning after they slept together, he showed them to her. She stared at them without saying a word. He got up to pee, and when he came back, she was dressed, standing at the door. She pecked his cheek, and then was gone. She has ignored him all week since. Damien's mask has small eye holes, and he can't see well. Tom McKiernan, the scum, stands in the hall and Damien accidently bumps him, spilling his beer. "Asshole," says Tom, but Damien just keeps walking. He is not sure if it was the drunken night of love or the sketches themselves that have caused Roxanne to snub him. Damien is not in love with Roxanne, but that doesn't temper this rejection any. He is in love with Melinda, but that is a whole different story. Melinda does not live in this town anymore, goes to a different school now and rarely returns his calls or letters, not because of any disgust so much as just general indifference. College is about more than finding love; it is about more than sex, it is about more than choosing the ONE and ONLY career path. In an astronomy class he learned about the stars and how when you see them, because of the speed in which light travels and how very very very—trillions of miles!—distant are those stars, you are looking not at what is but what was. Roxanne meets his eyes, and he waves quickly, but she narrows her eyes, looks away. She is talking to one of the soccer players, a business major who looks like the lead singer from Tears for Fears and who is dressed like Indiana Jones, whip and all. Damien is not an athlete, he has no major and the women who sleep with him don't talk to him after. Suddenly he does not want to be at this party, he wants to be outside, under stars and so he leaves the party alone and makes his way past the dorms, past the admin building, off campus, down a neighborhood block where a few straggling trick-or-treaters hustle the night's last candy. It is cold, and

Damien wears no jacket. He feels the sting on his skin, can taste his breath, the sour taste of it, the smell of sweat, and ferment, and hard plastic.

This morning, early, he couldn't sleep, so he was out walking then, too, watching the stars then, too. Different stars? These same stars? He's not sure; other than the big dipper, he can never keep them straight. He watched them as they melted into the bright light of dawn, and he remembered the way it felt the night he first kissed Melinda in the snow the year before, that bench by the pond, the slow glide of the swans. He lay in bed alone that night, imagining her next to him, imagined them together that night and the next night and the next night forever, but then this fall she did not return, went instead to a college three hundred and seventeen miles away, and he doesn't always feel this way, but this morning he felt stuck here, felt destined to stay forever in the impending snow, the touch of her lips still impressed upon his the only relief from the coming freeze. He sensed then how slowly everything breaks down, leads toward a slow and cold end. He feared a long future of nights alone in a trailer kitchen, cold hands wrapped around a coffee cup, the wind moving through a grill above a stove, a middle-aged man dwelling on old haunts, superficial love, gray winter skies. For what is love he wonders, but breath on a window pane, snow balanced on an oak branch before a breeze?

He removes his mask, throws it into a row of hedges, makes his way to the high school track further down the block. He starts running, and there are hurdles, hurdles and he jumps, sprints, feels the sweat, trades that warmth for the lone chill he knows will follow. He closes his eyes each time he jumps. Once, his heel taps a hurdle, but he does not tumble, maintains his balance and keeps running, around and around the track in a college town on a landmass on a planet that is slowly spinning and revolving in a universe where somewhere, trillions of miles away, a light, a single light among billions, travels steadily closer.

Let Your Breathing Return to Normal

"I'M GOING TO reinvent myself," says Karen. She's wearing the torn gray Nuggets sweatshirt she bought at a game last year, matching yellow sweatpants. The woman on the videocassette is dressed in white. The yoga lady. They are each barefoot. It's six o'clock in the morning.

"Reinvent yourself," I say.

"Yep," she says.

"Again," I say.

"I'm getting it right this time," she says.

She is down on hands and toes now, her ass in the air, a pose that I hear Yoga Lady call *downward facing dog*. It invites comments, but I keep them to myself on account of the fights Karen and I have been having lately, all of which seem to circle back to an alleged lack of maturity on my part. She doesn't say so, but I know it's an accusation fueled by the fact I haven't asked her to marry me. She's restless. But we've only been living together for going on two years now.

Let your breathing return to normal says the yoga lady. Karen stands and I feel her tension release as I walk out of the room and into the adjoining kitchen.

It's probable the new and improved Karen won't include me. She's considering moving to Tucson where her sister lives with an architect husband. I know this not because Karen's told me, but because her friend Lindee has. I slept with

Lindee once. It was a mistake. I mean, it was before Karen and I moved in together, but still.

Lindee and Karen work together. Every Thursday the three of us meet at the Rock Bottom for happy hour, and I drink whiskey sours and listen to them talk about people I don't know. Last week, Lindee and I arrived first. That's when she told me.

"Tucson," I said.

"What are you going to do about it?" Lindee wanted to know.

It was a good question. Before I could answer, Karen walked in the door.

I MET KAREN at a First Presbyterian Church Social on a Friday night. Since moving to Denver, I had tried meds, therapy, Rolfing, hypnosis and acupuncture before I started visiting churches, one Sunday at a time. I finally settled into First Pres, where I found the people as a rule the most laid back, the least pretentious. They didn't play with snakes, for example, or drink strychnine. They didn't volunteer you for Saturday night bake sales. There was no confession or penance. They went light on the fire and brimstone. All in all, they treated low level sin as a part of the human condition rather than a failing of the human spirit, and on God's great tests, they seemed pretty well content with low C's. It all felt like a rare world I might fit into. During the first sermon I attended, Reverend Tompkins, a baby-faced man with red hair and an impish grin, stated that perhaps God gave us football to keep us from working on the Sabbath. I felt certain I'd found the church for me.

Karen, whose history includes four engagements and zero marriages, was there each Sunday, third pew on the left, wearing the same blue dress with the white polka dots, her long blonde hair shining in the stained-glass morning. She always sat alone, and I watched her from my perch in the church balcony, doing my best to will only wholesome thoughts. That was important to me then, a phase. After every service, I waited and watched until she rose and walked slowly up the aisle, never once raising her eyes toward me.

I attended the social on that Friday night with the idea that she might be there, and when I arrived, there she was, drinking red punch and eating Lorna Doones, standing on the gymnasium floor. I walked up and introduced myself.

"So are you here for the Kool-Aid," she said raising her clear plastic cup, "or did you come to meet chicks?"

"I came to meet you," I said with a chivalrous grin that would have caused the more jaded to roll their eyes, but she smiled, looked down and blushed.

That was three years ago. Reverend Tompkins has since moved his family to a small town in Texas. The guy that replaced him had a lot of big ideas. Congregation volunteerism was big on the list. Living in sin wasn't. This he made clear to both Karen and me, and he gave us a choice. We chose sin. Karen goes to a Methodist church now. Sunday mornings, I sleep in.

Seventeen times and counting, in the last month, starting from the night Lindee told me about Tucson, Karen's asked me this question: "What is *wrong* with you?" She asks like it's the last piece of the puzzle, like once she figures it out, she'll be ready to go to Arizona and never repeat the same mistakes there. I hope she fills me in, because I'd like to know, too. I've got my own mistakes I'm trying not to repeat.

•

IN THE KITCHEN, a digital clock flashes an incorrect time. Toast crumbs are scattered across the counter, a tea-stained cup rests in the sink. The coffee pot sits lifeless and empty, a relic from Karen's pre-health-kick days.

"Are we out of coffee?" I ask.

"In the freezer," she says.

"Of course," I say. I open the freezer door. The coffee is an unfamiliar brand, in a small package with a colorful jungle scene on the front. "What kind of coffee is this?"

"It's organic," she says.

And decaf, I note. "Whatever happened to just plain old coffee?" I mumble.

"They still sell it," she says. "At a supermarket near you." She is lying flat on her back, her legs up against the fireplace wall.

Our apartment is a one bedroom with a view of the parking lot on one side, and the residential neighborhood beyond. Unused bicycles rest against balcony rails like animals in cages, listless, resigned to their fate.

I jumped out of an airplane once. It was shortly after I moved here. There were four of us. Joel and Katy were friends from college. Joel, who's since moved on to a better firm, got me the job I have now. Rebecca was from Scotland, and worked with Katy at the hospital. Later, Rebecca and I had a short-lived but intense romance—late nights dancing and drinking at a club called Orion, concerts at Fiddler's Green, sex on park benches, in parking lots, in a hotel hot tub.

The morning we skydived, I was the first to jump. I stood at the airplane door, looking down at the ground seven thousand feet below, our instructor yelling final instructions, trying to be heard over the engine and the wind. I got faint, dizzy, nauseous. I closed my eyes and jumped. I couldn't hear my screams so much as feel them rushing like dry vomit from my lips, and then I pulled the cord. I felt my body release like air from a balloon, I caught my breath, and I descended slowly to the ground.

Karen laughs when I tell her that story. "I can't believe *you* jumped out of an airplane," she says.

I imagine she uses it to defend me to her friends. "He sky-dives, you know," she tells them. "Or, at least he did once."

When I first moved to Denver, I was fresh out of college and never spent a weekend indoors. I had friends then. We backpacked in the Sangres, or the San Juans, the mountain pine forests cradling us as we slept at night; bicycled on the Colorado Trail, stopping to watch deer and elk along the way; rafted the Rio Grande, the whitewater carrying us ever forward. We went to outdoor music and art festivals, or bars at night, or house parties thrown by people we barely knew.

Joel and Katy have two kids now. I see them at summer barbecues, New Years. Rebecca, last I heard, is in Eugene and medical school. I spend my weekends at home, reading formulaic lawyer novels and watching Rockies pitchers raising their ERA's. I wonder about heaven, if my father's up there, looking down. I wonder if he's proud of me at all. I wonder if he can see that I haven't accomplished any of the things we used to talk about.

At the bathroom sink I cut myself shaving, drawing a thin line of blood beneath my right eye. The bleeding won't stop, so I cover it with Vaseline. I shower and dress, my once-favorite navy blue shirt faded. On the dresser is an old picture of myself from a camping trip, lying in a hammock between two trees in a green forest, young, smiling. Handsome, maybe even. In the background, a tent stands pitched next to a narrow stream. I have a beer in one hand, and with the other I'm petting Aspen, my old golden retriever. Now, I place black framed glasses on my face, look at a reflection in the mirror that I hardly recognize.

I work in an office, in payroll. I majored in political science at a small college in Pennsylvania, the idea once being that I would go to law school. Prestige, money, fenced community. Defending the powerless against the corrupt. That was the plan. Only I never got accepted. Anywhere. I had a solid GPA, but the LSAT exam was a bewildering maze I could never quite master.

From outside, light shows through the curtain's edges. The clock shows twelve minutes to the hour. Work is a twenty-minute drive away.

"What happened to your eye?" Karen asks as we say goodbye at the door.

"It's a new look," I say. "I'm reinventing myself."

THE SUN TREMBLES in a clear sky. When I seek peace to calm the anxiety, like now, I think about rain. I think about the time I was fifteen. A warm summer day, and I was running in the rain, past the corner convenience store, through the park, all the way to my friend Tina's house on 36th Street where we'd eat Heyday cookies and drink lemonade from a cowboy boot glass in her parents' basement. When the rain stopped we'd walk to the woods at the end of her road, climb to the top of a hill where we could look out over the highway below, the city in the distance.

I want a storm so bad sometimes. Rain, it seems to me, is a remnant from the past.

ON THE WAY to work, I stop for coffee at Java-the-Hut, a drive-through. The line is long. Finally, I give up and swerve out of the lane and back into traffic. James Taylor is on the radio, singing that song about *his* Karen: the silver sun. The lights all turn red as I approach.

By the time I get to the office, I'm eighteen minutes late, and I sneak quietly toward my cubicle, which, were you to see it from above, stands like a dead end in a rat maze. I scan the room for A.J., my manager. Then I see him, on the phone looking out his glass office. He wears a tailored gray suit with a lavender shirt and silk tie. His short brown hair is perfectly trimmed. His dark eyes meet mine. He doesn't smile.

"You, okay?" asks Jackson, coming up behind me. "You don't look good. You look disheveled."

"*Disheveled?* You been listening to vocabulary lessons on your way to work again?" I say.

"No, I'm serious, you really look bad," he says, following me into my cubicle.

"Really, I'm fine," I say. "I need coffee."

Then Brad enters. Short fat, four-eyed Brad. Because my cubicle is the dead end for the rats who never get conditioned properly.

"Anybody else moving up that corporate ladder today?" he asks, as he drops a thick file onto my desk. We ignore him.

"I wonder if you should, like, see a doctor or something," says Jackson.

"Why? What's wrong with you?" asks Brad.

"There's nothing wrong with me," I say.

They both follow as I walk across the aisle to the coffee maker. There is one pot, half full, nothing but clear hot water.

"What's this?" I ask.

"We're drinking tea today. All out of coffee. No one remembered to replace it," says Jackson.

"Try the peppermint," says Brad. "It's not bad."

"Shit," I say, and I crunch an empty Styrofoam cup in my hand. *Caffeineless in Denver*, I think. A horror flick. Coming to a theater near you.

"Get this," Brad says, reading from his cell phone. "These people paid some cult half a million dollars to clone their dead daughter. The cult claims it can duplicate the child— bring her back to life."

"They can do that, you know," says Jackson.

"You know what this means, don't you," says Brad.

"What does it mean, Brad?" I ask.

"That every day we're less irreplaceable," he says. "Even by our own parents."

I can feel the headache coming.

"I need coffee," I say.

"Wish someone'd clone me," says Brad, heading back to his own cubicle.

"What happened to your eye?" asks Jackson.

"Barroom brawl," I say.

"I mean it. I'm really worried about you," he says.

•

ON THE LAST day of every month, and then again on every fifteenth, like today, I do payroll, except this time, as I'm entering the data, my computer freezes. Again. This company's not exactly state-of-the-art. Like, for example, we don't have a built in backup drive—have to do it manually. I push about thirty keys, try a few combinations, instead of asking for tech help, like I know I'm supposed to "right away, before you scratch your balls or blink your eyes," A.J. had said when he trained me. His idea of management-speak. Then I turn the computer off, and wait for it to reboot, which has always worked in the past.

Only it never reboots. The screen comes up blank, nothing but a single flashing curser, and by that time I'm worried enough to call tech on their 1-800 line, which means I'm on hold for twenty minutes.

"Boy, that doesn't sound good," says an unconcerned voice at the other end of the line. He has me try a few prompts, load an old boot disk, neither of which works, and then he says, "I think your hard drive may have crashed. You may need to take your back-up file and use a different computer."

I look out the window. We are ten floors up. I look out at the street below, cars parked in the lots, people walking in fervent strides, a siren in the distance. I think, then, of the question no one ever dares ask: And if the parachute doesn't open?

"Back-up file?" I say.

Bottom line? An office full of people already behind on their bills don't get paid on time, and I'm this week's symbol of corporate incompetence with a great big target on my ass.

Not yet ten o'clock, and I'm in A.J.'s office, like a schoolboy before the principal. His jacket is draped on the back of a chair in the corner, and his sleeves are rolled up. On his desk rests a framed picture of his smiling wife, and two destined-for-greatness children.

"Okay," he says. "First of all, you're not being fired." Says this like he's the god of damage control, as if he stood up to the bigwigs and defended my case. "You have to understand, though, that we have policy and tech is here for a reason. They have a difficult enough job without us"—*us* he says, like we're in this together—"making it worse. And, damn it, you gotta' back up the files. That's like....I shouldn't even have to tell you that."

"I know," I say.

"You never think these things will happen to you," says A.J., shaking his head. "Now you know. It happens."

I laugh. I can't help it. When he looks at me with narrowed eyes, I laugh even harder. Because *you never think these things will happen to you* is what you say when someone gets cancer, or when someone close has been in an accident and died. And it just strikes me as absurd, A.J.'s comment, the payroll, Karen's yoga, my whole life. I can't even balance my checkbook, and I'm doing payroll? I'm in charge of paychecks? It doesn't even make sense. These people *deserve* the trouble I've caused. What am I doing here?

A.J. walks to his window, looks out, shakes his head. He glares at me. "This is not funny," he says.

"It won't happen again," I say.

"Make sure of it," he says, and when he turns back to look out the window, I get up and walk out of his office.

I spend the rest of the afternoon enduring co-workers' angry comments and glares, carefully re-entering data into the system.

"Thanks a lot, Einstein," says Brad as he passes, on his way out the door. By 6:30, I'm just starting to compile the data, and re-enter it onto the system. A.J. and I are the only ones left in the office.

"Long day, huh?" he says. "How's it going?"

"Couple more hours, I think," I say. I don't look up.

"Well...," he says. But he never finishes. And then I can hear him walking away. I try to muster some level of hate for him, but I can't.

It was on a Thursday, that night I slept with Lindee. I'd been dating Karen for about six weeks, but she was away, visiting family in Omaha. We were at the Rock Bottom. It'd been a rough week, mostly on account of Aspen dying. He was sixteen, and I'd had him since he was a pup. He'd been arthritic for the last couple of years—wouldn't even walk up the stairs to sleep in my room anymore. He lay down on his mat in the kitchen of the house I was living in at the time, and for two days wouldn't eat, his eyes glossed over, his heartbeat slow and labored. I took him to his longtime vet, a man named Dr. Hayne who loved Aspen almost as much as I did. Dr. Hayne had watery eyes when he told me there was nothing he could do. I slept with Aspen on the kitchen floor that night, his head cradled in my arms, his eyes fading, like a child trying to fight off sleep. In the morning—it was a Sunday—he was dead, and I sat against the wall, too numb to cry.

So Karen was away, and I was still hurting about Aspen, and there, sitting at the bar was Lindee, with her shoulder-cut brown hair, her blue eyes. She wore a white dress with a green and pink floral design. She'd recently had her nose pierced, and wore a silver stud, a fairly new trend then. She pointed at it.

"What do you think?" she asked.

To be honest, I've never been a fan of the whole piercing trend, but there was something about it—I don't know, it worked for her.

"Not bad," I said. When I told her about Aspen, she leaned forward and touched my hand. We drank, and we talked about music and books—she'd read Marquez and Carver and Annie Proulx's Wyoming stories. Lindee grew up here, and we talked about sports, how the Rockies were going downhill, the Broncos were rising. And we talked about Karen and love and relationships in general.

"Do you think you know when you're in love?" I asked her.

She gave me a puzzled look. "What do you mean?"

"I mean, if you meet someone, and enjoy their company, and everything is comfortable, nice, but..."

"Are you out of your mind?" she said. "Love is chaos, turmoil, like flying into the heart of a hurricane. It shakes you, and sends you out of control. You turn, and fall, and scream, and laugh. It's the best possible of all fears. When it's love, you know. Trust me." I've always wondered why she didn't follow up with the next logical question. *Haven't you ever felt that way?* But she just looked down at her drink, shook her head. I realize now that she didn't ask because she already understood the sad answer.

So, anyway. We were drunk, and I thought about Aspen, and I tried to hold them back, but the tears came anyway and I was embarrassed, and I turned away from her in my barstool, but she put her hand on my shoulder, and turned me back toward her, and she hugged me, and when we went to part, we looked at each other, and our lips touched and I can still feel the cotton texture of her dress, my hand on the small of her back.

None of which excuses what happened that night, of course, back at her small apartment with David Sanborn on the stereo and the moon outside her bedroom window.

"A one-time thing?" she'd asked the next morning.

"One time," I agreed. And every Thursday night since, when Karen and I say goodbye, Lindee and I hug, and I'm careful not to linger there in her arms, careful not to give myself away.

I STAY IN the office and re-enter the data. Get it all ready to submit for the issue of the checks. Checks may be delayed for one extra day, but the issue is mainly resolved. I will be the target of disgust for a few days. My name will be a verb. "Don't Martin it," they'll say. Or, "Man you really Martined that." Eventually, though, I'll be forgotten. Replaced. The whole inefficient world will just keep right on spinning. Brad, I think, would be perfect for this job. I leave a note for A.J.

I drive onto Auraria Parkway, and then through the downtown, passing two old men in dark jackets walking with canes, a group of women in business suits. A teenage couple—the boy with a studded collar, and black hair in a spike, the girl with barbed-wire tattooed on her arm—kiss furiously on a bench. On the sidewalk, pigeons compete for crumbs.

Through the side streets I drive, a turn left into an old neighborhood, houses in a mixed array of unkempt lawns and broken shutters alongside homes which are newly painted and remodeled. Old rusty Chevys are parked next to new Nissans.

I turn on the radio, flip through stations, finally settle on 101.5, KJZY, smooth jazz. It's going to be okay, I think. I'll get my shit together. Focus a little more. Ask Karen to marry me, get a house, another dog like Aspen. Kids maybe, and a garage. A two-car garage.

I drive into a newer neighborhood, the suburb homes resting quietly, all painted in bland colors—whites and grays and light blues—with garage doors that open automatically as residents arrive or leave, the green lawns all cut on Saturdays, flower beds well defined by railroad ties, sprinkler systems so smart, they know when it rains. I weave my way through, turn onto Colorado, then left, along the broad street with the daisy-patterned medians, and then right, into the apartment lot complex. Dinner, I think. A romantic dinner with Karen at Guiselli's, the dim lights, the mirrored walls reflecting old bottles, mandolin music in the background. I suddenly realize how hungry I am. It's almost nine o'clock.

I park my car and walk up the stairs.

"Karen?" I call when I turn the key and enter. But she isn't home. One of Karen's health magazines rests on the tiled coffee table. "One Hundred Ways to be Happy" offers the cover. I find the article and skim the list: pets, plants, vitamins, exercise. Fresh air. I flip on the TV. A familiar commercial. Richard Stans, attorney at law. The sound is off, but I know the words: *have you been injured in an automobile accident?* Richard can help. He will sue. He will get you the settlement you deserve. All you have to do is call, 1-800 yadda yadda.

It's easy to hate Stans, but he is a lawyer. And what am I?

•

I CHANGE, PULL a beer from the refrigerator, open the balcony door. Outside the air is cool, traffic hums, an engine turns over. I hear a sliding glass door from below; pop music I don't recognize comes streaming into the evening, the smell of barbecue charcoal burning. I look out at the buildings, the sun casting long shadows across the yard, the sun almost behind the mountains. A cricket chirps. I finish my beer. I should eat, or go to the bar, but I look out at the complex pool and decide to go for a swim instead. There's no beer allowed in the pool area, so I pour vodka in a plastic cup, and disguise it with orange juice. When Karen finds me less than an hour later, I am drunkenly splashing a backstroke.

"Hey," I say, when I see her standing at the water's edge.

She just shakes her head, sits down in one of the deck chairs. I try to pull myself up at the wall, but my hand slips, and I bump my chin on the concrete. So I move to the ladder, climb it, and walk over and sit down beside her.

"Marry me," I say.

For a long time, she doesn't look at me, but gazes out over the water, which is neon green in the light.

"We have to talk," she says. I nod and look out across the pool to the parking lot. An elderly man I've seen before is pushing his wife in her wheelchair. "I put in my two week's notice," she says.

"When?" I ask.

She takes a deep breath. "Two weeks ago. Martin, I'm moving."

"Tucson," I say.

She nods. "I'm leaving tonight. I want to be amiable about this."

"Yes!" I say. "Let's be amiable. Skinny dip with me? We can get drunk, screw. Very amiable. A goodbye to end all goodbyes," I say.

She looks at me for a long time, bites her upper lip and shakes her head. "Do you know what your problem is?" she asks. "And I'm saying this to help you, so don't take it personally. You need to grow up a little. I mean, join the world of adults, you know."

"No," I say. "I'm going to resist it, fight it until the bitter end."

She sighs. "Except that it's something you can't fight. It will only make you bitter in the end."

"I quit my job today too," I say. "No two weeks' notice. Just up and left."

She nods, as if not surprised. I'd hoped for more of a reaction. "Everything is going to work out for each of us," she says. "I can feel it." She gets up, leans down and presses both lips against my forehead, says, "I have to go pack now."

I watch her as she walks across the grass to our apartment, and I wonder whether love is a smooth glider ride through a clear sky, or chaos, turmoil, like flying into the heart of a hurricane where you are shaken, and sent out of control twisting, falling, screaming, laughing. Almost thirty, and I so want to feel all the things I never have.

I HAVEN'T BEEN home to Philly for seven years now, not since my father's funeral. One of the last times I saw him, we spent a late night talking, the clot fresh and visible on his arm as he sat across from me in his leather chair, and he spoke of his days in the city, drinking with friends at a downtown lounge called McGillin's, making the contacts there that would get him his first job. Later he would live in a house with two other men—just before he met my mother—and they would have parties on weekends. I conjured the old pictures of him as a young man, tried to imagine him and his friends, music and laughter, their whole life ahead of them, and he spoke of working in an office with no air-conditioning and the sweat rolling down his arms onto the papers, wind gusts coming through the open windows blowing the papers around the room. And then he had a life filled with love, and children and a job that served him well. What is wrong with me   what is wrong with me   what is wrong with me   What is wrong with me is that I *do* want to join the adult world, I'm not trying to fight it at all, I'm fighting to join it, and I want to live up to the life he set me up for, him and others like him, a whole generation who lived by rules that no longer make the same sense, and yet I crave them, and I fear love as I fear death and each day I feel the weight of gravity more and more and more.

I walk to our apartment, watch Karen pack. "I'll be back in a couple weeks for the rest of my stuff," she says, setting a large suitcase by the door.

"Don't go," I say.

She looks up at me, shakes her head. She is not crying, and I wish that she were. "I appreciate you saying that, but we both know you don't mean it. I'm going to leave now," she says. "I like to drive through to the morning." She looks at me, smiles sadly. She says, "I loved you once, I really did," and she walks out the door, down the steps. I hear the car door close, the engine start. It is dark now. I can hear I-25 traffic.

And I don't know what to do, only know that I can't be here, that I must move, that I am in no condition to drive a car. I walk out to the balcony, pull my mountain bike inside, and then carry it out the front door and down the steps. I begin to ride. I don't have a light on the bike, but I pedal on side streets, beneath street lights. I head west, and then north.

I am on a trail that runs through a park. There are street-lights, but under the shade of trees, it is dark. I am pedaling, pedaling, spinning my pedals as fast as I can. Where are you, Dad, when I need you most? I was a boy, and it was fall. We had driven to the Poconos. The crunch of leaves beneath the trees. We walked on a trail, and you taught me the names of trees—oak, birch, maple. I thought you would always be here, that I might always walk beside you. Karen is driving now, I see her at a filling station, fueling her escape, blowing the hair out of her face, standing beneath the fluorescent glow looking out at the silhouetted mountain and Jupiter beyond. I ped-al faster and think of A.J., wonder what he'll think of me in the morning. The truth is, I like him. There's a lot about A.J worthy of admiration. I should be more like A.J., and I pedal and pedal, more responsible, I pedal, more stable, pedal, more sober, more decent, more.

A sickening creak, a halting beneath me, I am falling, and there is pavement against my face, my side. I go to push myself from the ground and pain shoots from my palm to my right elbow. I roll to my other side, push myself up with my left hand. I touch my hand to my knee and there is blood. I stand, return to my bicycle, which is leaning at an awkward angle, the front tire stuck in a street grate. I lift it out with my left hand, try to roll it down the street, but the rim is bent, the tire won't roll. I stand panting. Disgusted, I shove the bike to the side of the road and start to walk. New pains reveal themselves as my adrenaline slows. My knee aches. I touch my face and feel the sandpaper scrape, the blood. Where am I? I try to place myself, but don't recognize the neighborhood. I look at the stars, try to remember the words of an astronomy professor I had once, but can't remember how to navigate.

In a gravel alley that separates the houses on two separate streets, dogs bark as I lurk along the wooden fences. I decide to cut through a yard, to get to the street on the front side of the houses, so I climb over a fence.

And then I am running, across the yard, my footsteps splattering the damp grass, down a short hill, and I fall, ass over teakettle, spinning in the darkness, my clothes wet, mud and grass on the front of my shirt. A light comes on from the house, I hear a screen door open, and I jump up, run to the front of the yard, the other end of the fence, climb over it, spilling my body into high weeds and soil, and I hear footsteps on a wood balcony, and a voice from the house hollers, they have a gun, they'll call the police, and I imagine the people inside the house, hope that they won't feel forever violated. I want them to know, I am not a threat. If I stopped to explain, maybe they would understand, but how would I explain? So with a limp I am running, and I make it to the end of the street, through a school yard nearby, the dark blur of night, suburban streetlights, traffic, a distant siren. A car approaches on the road, and I hide behind a shrub, waiting for it to pass.

When the car passes, I listen intently. The night is silent.

I continue through neighborhoods, hiding from traffic,

hiding for reasons I don't understand, until finally, I find a strip mall, and a pay phone in a parking lot.

Instinctively, I dial the first six numbers of my own apartment, before I remember that Karen won't be there. Then, I hang up. It's nearly one in the morning now. Who are your friends at a time like this? Jackson, maybe, or Brad, or Joel and Katy? No, and no and no.

I put two coins in the phone and dial. I have the number memorized, though I have never dialed it before. It rings seven times. Finally, a drowsy voice answers.

"Can you come pick me up?" I say.

"I'm on my way," she says. I sit on the curb of the parking lot, outside an office for lease, and wait. In less than 15 minutes, Lindee is there.

"What happened to you?" she wants to know as I get in the car.

"It's a long story," I say.

"Are you okay?" she asks looking at my mud-and-grass-stained jeans.

"No," I say. "I don't think that I am."

She takes me back to her apartment, where she cleans the mud from my arms, disinfects the scrapes on my elbows, places band-aids on them.

"How could you be so stupid?" she asks.

It's a good question, so I attempt an answer, and I talk and talk and talk. She listens and nods, sips her coffee. Smiles when I am funny, purses her lips in sympathy when I speak of my father. When I stop talking she looks at me as if considering. And then she stands up and says, "Come on."

"Are you sure?" I ask.

She shrugs. "I get lonely sometimes." She smiles, walks into her bedroom. I follow.

After, I realize I have known what I wanted all along, and it surprises me how big the difference can be between how we see our lives and how they really are, and she holds me, falls asleep in my arms. I look at the clock on her nightstand. It says two forty-seven, in small digital red numbers. A hurricane, I think. Definitely like flying into the eye of a hurricane.

I lie in bed and think about TV ad lawyers, their eight hundred numbers and shady promises. I think about plummeting downward through the sky. Let your breathing return to normal, I think. Later, that morning we will rise and she will drive me home. I will not show up to work. I will return disheveled to my apartment, where Karen's parking spot will sit vacant. Once inside, I will stand before a half-empty closet. I will place a filter in the coffee pot, and watch silently as the hot organic coffee falls, one steady drip at a time.

Skinning Wolverines

GARY HAD NO business driving out on the ice that night, and maybe he knew it, maybe he understood his own psyche enough to see the evil in the things that he'd done, and maybe he understood us, too, Rudy and me, knew that the only men who could've saved him wouldn't. I tell myself that what happened, how it all played out, was necessary, inevitable. Was it right what we did, or, I should say, what we didn't do? I've replayed it in my head a million times. It would've been dangerous, going out on that ice, but, as anyone who knows me can tell you, I've never been one hindered by fear, have always been a man of action. Vengeance or justice? I go back and forth. Anyone who'd been living in Kakarak village during those months knew something had to be done, understood it was Gary's own ignorance that did him in. He was hell bent on destruction, both self-wise and other, was heading toward one of those tragedies you read about.

And yet, later, when it was over, the night merged into morning, and we had awakened to that sun coming over the frozen lake, I felt a remorse I didn't expect, and as I rode across that ice on my snow machine back home, I felt a nausea, a shivering cold that had nothing to do with the snow and ice of winter. I got back, and told Stephanie what happened, and she gave me that look, and I felt her horror, felt the weight of what I'd let happen, understood then what I was capable of.

•

THE WEEK HAD started innocently enough. Monday, I'd been home drinking screwdrivers—except we were out of orange juice, so I'd used orange soda—minding my own business in my own living room on a late afternoon. There was an old Western on the TV. Stephanie was in the back room changing into her workout clothes. A fire burned in the wood stove. I'd just finished oiling a large wolverine fur, and I had it lying out on the kitchen table, drying beneath an electric fan. We lived in a modular duplex, district housing. The walls inside were paneled, photos of various hunting trips hung from a cork bulletin board on the wall. I was on the couch, shoes off, glad to be home after a typical day of madness at that school, when I heard the roar of a Honda four-wheeler coming around back. I knew it wasn't Deanna, the kindergarten teacher and village loudmouth, usually the only other person who'd drive behind the place. I could tell. I knew every motor in that village by sound. I knew who it was, and I wasn't' thrilled. There were two-hundred people living in that village. For the most part, I liked a hundred and ninety-nine of them.

Gary was the odd man out.

I waited for the halting of the engine, the heavy steps from his boots on our back stairs.

I turned down the volume on the TV, but what was I going to do, cower in my house all day? So I answered when he knocked, tried to look busy, like I was in the middle of something real important. Opened the door just a crack. That kind of thing. As if Gary had a clue in Hades about such social cues.

"We gotta get back up to the school. It's the generator again," he said. Said it like that was my job. The month before, in January, I'd spent three sleepless nights baby-sitting the village generator. Because, in village Alaska, if the generator quits, and you're not there firing it back up right away, it freezes on you, and then you have a real problem. January's not a good time to have a bad generator.

"I'll meet you," I said.

"Don't be long," he said.

GARY WAS THE principal at the school where I taught second grade. Stephanie and I worked in that village for thirteen years. It's a Native village, Athabascan. The only white people here are us teachers, and Eric, the health aid. During the time Steph and I have lived here, we saw a lot of teachers come and go. In thirteen years, Gary was our tenth principal. We've had our share of whack jobs, but this guy beat them all.

I used to joke about killing him. Stephanie would roll her eyes at such talk, but there were nights I lay awake thinking about it. One shot, that's all it would take. Let's face it, there are people in this world whose only contribution will come when they're under the ground, feeding the soil. I know how that must sound, now, but it's the truth, it's how I felt about Gary.

I know—you're thinking, hell, Henry, everyone hates their boss. Trust me. This was different.

WE HAD A principal, two before Gary, who was almost as bad. Lloyd Hermanson. Big fat guy, bald spot, curly gray on the sides. One day he was out behind our house with his shotgun dressed in fatigues. I mean, this is the kind of thing you deal with out here.

"The hell you doing?" I called out to him from my porch.

"Dogs," he said. "Too damn many of them." Stephanie's got a little fur ball of a mutt named Maggot that sometimes ran around out there.

"Get the hell away from here," I yelled at him. Hunting dogs. I mean, where do they find these people?

"STEPH," I CALLED out to her over the whir of her stay-young machine, a stationary bicycle, we mail-ordered from Sears. Cost more to ship than to buy the damn thing. "Gotta' go up to the school."

The machine stopped. "Why?" she asked.

"Generator's out."

"You ever say 'no'?" she said. But the whir began before I could smart back.

I pulled on my Carhartt jacket, my gloves, my handmade mink-skin hat, and walked out into the chill.

Outside, the sun had just set. Up here, you measure winter not by temperature, but by light. Across the frozen lake, Hoknede Mountain rested flat against a blue-gray sky. Saber-sized icicles still hung from our roof. The days were getting longer. Winter was retreating. If this school year ever ends, I remember thinking, it'll be a very good thing.

I had a general bad feeling about things around then. Like, that was the third time in less than a month the generator had gone out. The school van, one of only a handful of vehicles in the village, broke an axle. A freezer—the one with the next week's supply of cafeteria food, including chicken patties, corn dogs, hamburger—somehow got unplugged and everything thawed over the weekend, spoiling most of it. Put it this way:

there were about eight people who had keys to the school, and of those eight, only three had keys to the boiler room which is where the generator was. I'm one. Harold, the school maintenance guy was another, and, trust me, he's about as harmless as a squirrel.

That left Gary.

Why, you wonder, would Gary, or anyone, commit such acts? Because, flat and simple, he was pissed at the administration on account of they'd already told him he wasn't coming back, on account he was a nut case. Trust me, Gary had a bone to pick. I looked at that axle. Two things: one, it was solid steel—three men with sledge hammers couldn't have broken it. Two, at the break, unmistakable, was the blue discoloration of heat. As in blow torch.

"Must have got hot," he shrugged when I pointed it out to him. In Alaska. In February.

On my way to the school I stopped at Keith's house. He was a new teacher then—he's since moved back outside, to sunny California. Still get Christmas cards, signed by his wife.

"Want to go up to the school?" I asked.

He laughed. "Let me guess. Generator?"

"You're pretty smart. You comin'?"

"Yeah. I left a book up there I need to get. Is our boy gonna be there?" he asked.

"He's in charge," I said.

"Yeah," said Keith. "Figure that one out. Get this: this morning, about three, I wake up. All I hear are pipes banging below my house. I mean, what the hell? All I could think of was one of your skinless wolverines, come back to life to haunt me. I should have known. This morning at school, he comes up to me and wants to know if I heard him this morning. I said what the hell were you doing? He was fixing my hot water heater, because I made the mistake of telling him that I was running out of hot water in the morning. I mean, I appreciate he fixed it, but three in the morning?"

"I told you," I said. "The man doesn't sleep."

KEITH WAS THERE in the first place because two other teachers, Jared and Kelli, left. Gary pretty much chased them off by October. Not a great loss to be honest with you. East Coast liberal arts teacher college doesn't prepare you for the Alaskan bush. Even without Gary's bullshit they wouldn't have lasted more than a year. What did he do? He bullied them, for one. He yelled at them in front of students, at faculty meetings. He tried to force them into separate housing (technically, I guess they weren't married). The house he tried to arrange for her didn't even have locks on the door. She told Stephanie that he told her she was too good for Jared, smiled when he said it, creeped her out. One morning, he woke Jared at four o'clock, told him to go plow the school parking lot. Then, after Jared left—this according to Kelli—Gary stayed and helped himself to coffee; was sitting there at the table when she walked out of the bedroom to get in the shower. Sometimes, they'd look out their window, and Gary would be out there looking in, the creep. I'll tell you, I put shades on all our windows. Anyway, none of us were surprised when we came in one Monday and Kelli and Jared were both gone. Sacrificed their Alaska license for good, chartered a flight, disappeared. E-mailed their resignation. The geniuses at administration, which is two hundred air miles away, decided to not even replace Kelli. To fill Jared's spot, they hired Keith.

Keith was different, tough for a city boy. His only issue was a wife that lived in Anchorage. All he talked about was missing her, as if his coming to that village wasn't a choice. But I liked him. I knew he'd be okay after one morning in the office. He had already been there a couple weeks by then. It was early, before school. We were in the office drinking coffee, me, Keith, and Eric, because he was there dropping off his wife who taught sixth grade. Anyway, Gary came in on one of his tirades.

"I'm gonna' be in a bad mood today," he said angrily. We all looked at each other and shrugged. So what else was new. Then he kicked a chair across the room. It flew over the table behind us, and smashed against the wall, just missing the large plate office window. I looked at Keith, to see what his reaction to *that* drama would be. He calmly sipped his coffee. When Gary stormed out of the office, Keith looked at the chair, looked back at us, shook his head.

"Wide left," he said.

I HAVE TWO rules I live by: What doesn't kill you will make you stronger, and never take a knife to a gunfight. That village had changed a lot by then, since we first got there. Man, do I remember that day. August, 1987. We landed on the small air strip, and unloaded all our stuff—a year's worth of belongings. There was supposed to be someone to pick us up, according to the district people. But of course there wasn't. After about twenty minutes, a man pulled up on his Honda. Finally, I thought. But he just looked at us, spat on the ground, and took off. So we walked, dragging our bags and boxes behind us. We got around the corner, and there was a sign, *Welcome to Kakarak*. Except Kakarak had been crossed out with spray paint, and someone had written the word *HELL* in big black letters. Then, we finally got to the house the district provided for us, and across the front was painted the words "Go home honkees." Spelled with two e's. One night, early in that year, two of the village men showed up outside. They were drunk and they had guns. They started shooting into the air. I knew it was just to scare us, but we slept in our bathtub anyway, that night, and the next night, too.

At school, the kids gave us hell. Stephanie taught high school, and those kids treated her bad. They cursed her, called her names. Refused to listen, wouldn't do the work. Threatened her. She cried about every night that first year. But when I suggested we leave, she wouldn't hear of it.

"No one's chasing me away," she said.

One day, we were coming home from school on our Honda, and there was a man in the road. Irvin Balluta. Irvin and I are actually pretty good friends now. I mean, I don't hold a grudge. How would you like strangers coming to your town, telling you what you need to know to function in their world? You'd resent it, too. That day, though, Irvin had a gun, was coming back from hunting caribou. Anyway, he saw us coming and raised the gun, big grin on his face, thinking he'd scare us. I grew up in Montana. You don't point guns at people. I punched the gas, and before he could jump out of the way, I clothes-lined him, knocking him sideways. The gun flew out of his hands and landed on the other side of the road. I stopped, got off, picked up the gun. It was empty like

I knew it would be. I threw it as far as I could, down toward the lakeshore. I got back on the Honda, and rode away. Never said a word to him.

Word musta' got around. After that, people started leaving us alone.

Thirteen years we stuck it out. By then, people treated us with respect, admiration even. When Keith came in, no one gave him much grief at all. Except, of course, for Gary.

So, KEITH AND I rode up to school, and Gary was lying on the ground, monkey wrench in one hand, Phillips screwdriver in the other. Keith looked at me, eyebrows raised. There was nothing anywhere near the ground that needed work on that generator. I walked over, looked at the gauges, flipped a switch, fired it up. Worked like a charm.

Gary stood up, brushed himself off. "Sometimes," he said, "you get a couple of those bolts on the bottom loose, and it throws it out of whack. Guess that did it. You guys eat yet?"

"Yeah," said Keith. "Already ate," though I knew he hadn't.

"Hey, how'd your trap lines check out this weekend?" Gary asked me.

"Empty," I said. He shook his head, like he would have done better.

THE TRUTH WAS, my lines had checked out pretty well. Beneath my house just then, in the crawl space, were seventeen skinned wolverine carcasses. In that state, they looked almost human, like babies.

"Jeez, Henry," Keith had said when I showed him. "It's like *Silence of the Lambs* down there."

On weekends, I used to take Stephanie and Maggot on our snow-machine, and head up the lake. I have a buddy, caretakes a lodge up there. Rudy. The Mad Russian. He calls me Bigfoot on account of my size sixteens. That was us: Bigfoot and the Mad Russian, trapping in the snow.

It was the greatest thing in the world, riding a snow-machine around there in the winter. You got on that ice and just flew. Your eyes watered in the cold wind, and the world became one impressionistic blur. Imagine Monet, if he'd been Yupik, saw you, put you in his art. At dusk, the pink alpenglow reflected on the ice-covered lake. Sometimes there were caribou out there.

Rudy and I ran a trap line. Fox, lynx. Mostly wolverines. I miss Rudy, wish we were both better about staying in touch. Does he wonder if we'd done the right thing that night? I asked him once. He just glared at me.

"That man," he said, "had no right to put us in the position to have to decide. What happened, he done. We had nothing to do with it one way or the other."

One Saturday, long before that night, we had a wolverine in a trap. Man, was it pissed. Snarling and hissing, murder in his eyes. I walked toward him, my pistol pointed, when I saw something that sent a chill up my spine. Namely, that the trap was barely holding the wolverine by the edge of his foot. Then, because I'm about a hundred points shy of a genius IQ, as evidenced by the fact that I left my snowshoes on the snow machine, I took a step into what I thought was shallow snow, and suddenly found myself in a drift, buried to my shoulders.

Then the wolverine broke lose from the trap.

Let me tell you about wolverines. They're the toughest

son-bitches in the world, and the meanest. You, me, just about any other species on the planet, we've been caught in a trap, approached by a man with a gun. We get loose, we're high-tailing our ass. But not a wolverine. A wolverine's all fight and no fear. So he comes at me, full sprint, teeth bared, aiming for my neck. I'm desperately trying to lift my arm with the gun in it, but I'm stuck. This is it, I think.

Finally, I hear a gun shot from behind me. Then another. Another. At last, about ten feet from my face, Rudy drops him.

"Geez, Rudy," I said as he helped pull me from the snow. "What were you waiting for?"

"You were in my line of fire," he said as he put a pinch of Copenhagen behind his lip. "I had to get a better angle."

"Damn you, " I told him after he'd dug me out of the snow, and we inspected our kill. "You ruined the pelt." But I was grateful. Man, was I grateful.

AFTER GARY LEFT the boiler room, Keith and I went into the school building so he could grab the book from his classroom. I walked into the school office, checked my mailbox, skimmed through a catalog. The steady static of the radio filled the room. The radio was village Alaska's primary source for communication. For those who had one, it was like a village-wide intercom system. You could even buy hand-held types to carry on your snow machines and Hondas. "Randy Trefon," said a female voice over the crackling of static. "We're eating. Get your butt home."

I walked out of the office. From downstairs, I heard running water. I was thinking someone left the water on in the boys' bathroom, so I walked down. I took one step into the bathroom and almost landed on my ass, because the floor was flooded. Not only was the water running full blast, but the drain had been clogged with a wad of green Play-Doh.

"That son-of-a-bitch," I said. I cleaned out the drain, and Keith helped me mop up.

"What next?" I said.

"Something," said Keith.

"COME IN FOR a snort?" asked Keith when I dropped him off.

"Sure," I said.

Inside, his house was bare. There were a few books on the shelves, a picture of his wife on the mantle. The walls were plain, the carpet beige. When he opened the refrigerator, I saw one pitcher of water and one of orange juice. Other than that, it was empty.

He pulled a bottle of vodka from the cabinet above the stove, mixed two screwdrivers, half and half. Another reason I liked Keith—he never mixed a weak drink.

"That man," he said, "was not meant to lead."

"We have a serious Gary problem," I said.

"He's so dumb, he thinks a Volvo is part of a woman's anatomy," said Keith.

"You're so dumb, it takes you two hours to watch 60 Minutes," I said. "I could kill him. It would be easy. No guilt. I'd be doing the world a service."

"You're such a redneck, you think a six-pack and a bug zapper is a high form of entertainment," said Keith.

"That's true. I like to watch 'em fry," I said.

"If Gary was murdered, the first place everyone would

look would be in your crawl space with all the other dead bodies," said Keith.

"Hell, Keith, no one would look. And even if they found him, I'd be a hero. I'm telling you, I'd be doing us all a favor. Last week I had to talk Ilene out of quitting. That place would fall down if she quit, trust me."

"Why was she going to quit?" he asked.

"Gary. He keeps showing up at her door, wanting to come in, at all hours of the night. He told her he's in love with her."

"Isn't she married?" Keith asked.

"Yes, but her husband works up at the slope at Prudhoe Bay. So Gary keeps showing up. Tells her he wants to take care of her." I took a long drink from my glass "Did you see those flowers in the office today? They were from Gary. Had them flown in. He asked her if he could move in with her. When she said no, he asked her if he could pitch a tent in her yard."

"You're making this up," said Keith.

"I'm not," I said. I pulled back the curtain and peered out the window. It had grown dark. Stars hung like glitter over the lake outside Keith's window. I'd been wondering about Keith lately. He seemed decent, and I liked him, but he was a long way from home. "Let me ask you something—what the hell are you doing here?"

Keith laughed. "I ask myself that question every day."

"I mean, you have a wife. Marriage is good, right?"

"Yeah," he said.

"There's got to be jobs in Anchorage. What the hell?"

"There's no teaching jobs in Anchorage. I mean there are, but the hoops you have to jump through. Here, they're so desperate, they don't even do background checks. I subbed there.

Class sizes up to forty, worst behaved kids on the planet. It was chaos. After two weeks, I was ready to hang myself. And when they hired me for this job, they didn't tell me there was a psycho running the place."

"I still don't get it," I said.

He stood up to make us more drinks.

"You want to know the truth?" he said from the kitchen.

"No. Lie to me," I said.

"It's like this. My whole life I dreamt of coming to Alaska. Grizzly bears, igloos, bush planes. The whole bit. So, finally we have our chance. Melanie applies and gets a job. It's a job that has her flying all over the state, working in villages—a regular adventure. I don't have any such luck. I mean there's teaching jobs all over, but not in Anchorage. Hell, they wouldn't even send me a sub packet. Told me I had to come pick it up for myself. A little hard to do from Texas, which is where we were living when we decided to move. Anyway, we get up here and I'm working subbing, whatever. Meanwhile, Melanie's traveling all over Alaska. She's seeing caribou herds, working with Native people, the whole bit, and I'm living in a city, which, except for a few moose walking around, is pretty much like every other city in America. Strip malls, fast food, crime. I hated it. Then she'd come home and tell me these stories. I ached to see the things she was seeing, eat dried fish, meet Aleut elders, fly in bush planes. Comes right down to it, she was living my dream, and I was jealous as hell. So, I got my name on the state teacher placement list, and when I was offered this job, I grabbed it." He brought me my drink, handed it to me.

I laughed. "You're so dumb, you traded living with your

wife for working for Gary." I understood, though. When Stephanie and I first came to Alaska, we lived in Anchorage for a year. It was not fun. Anchorage is a city like any other — dirty, traffic, people living on the streets, crime, sirens all the time. Not the Alaska of anybody's dreams.

"Damn it!" said Keith.

"What?" I asked.

"The freakin' water. Scalded me."

And then I thought again of Gary, crawling around down there, when everyone else was sleeping. I'm telling you what. After so many times, you know. Those things weren't accidents.

So, HERE'S A mistake I made—something I regret mightily, and I can't help but think how it set up all that was to happen that night months later. Maybe everything comes down to fate, and the way things end up have less to do with the decisions made in the moment, than with those made earlier, before you can foresee the end result. That September, when everything was new again, and it seemed like there was hope in the world, I took Gary to Rudy's with me and Stephanie. Not that I wanted to. It was more like he invited himself. He asked me what I was doing for the weekend, and I told him.

"That sounds great. Hey, I'll go with you," he said. I should have balked then, told him that since it was Rudy's place, I really wasn't in a position to invite him, which would've been true. But he was my new boss, and he seemed, though odd, at least harmless, and I thought how the worst that could happen probably wouldn't, so I said, yeah, Gary, whatever. Come right the hell along.

The worst that could happen was worse than I thought. We spent the day checking trap lines, looking for moose, mostly just riding and enjoying the autumn air. At first, he was tolerable. Annoying, but tolerable. That night at the lodge was where the trouble began. We were drinking bloody Marys. Gary got stupid drunk, and started spouting off.

"Hey, you commie cocksucker," he said to Rudy, "Pour me another of those?" Rudy, who's among other things a Vietnam vet, just glared at him. Let's just say it was a poor choice of words. But, hey, Gary's life was built on poor choices.

That night revealed to us all one deeply disturbed mind. Like, for example, in detail he told us—right in front of Stephanie, the prick—what he would like to do with our school secretary, Ilene. Listen, what people do in their privacy is to each their own, but you don't discuss it in detail to people you've just met.

"Ilene's married," I said. Then I tried to change the topic, but to no avail.

"Her husband—I'm going to rescue her from that asshole, you just wait and see," he said. He went on to make vulgar remarks about two of our high school girls—girls I once had as second graders. You don't have to tell me about how men in hunting lodges talk. I'm an old pro at profanity and innuendo. This was beyond that. Stephanie, who knows me well, sported me one of her behave-yourself-Henry looks, but the guy I was worried about was Rudy, who just happens to have a nineteen-year-old daughter in Seattle. The prospect of guys like Gary in the world makes him crazy.

"Did you get me that drink yet?" Gary said to Rudy.

"You've got all you're getting," Rudy said between clenched

teeth. "You probably need to shut the hell up and go to bed, now." Then he got up and walked outside into the cool air.

Too stupid to even realize that what he'd said might offend someone, Gary shrugged and did what he was told. I walked out to join Rudy. The stars were out. In the distance, lake-water lapped against the rocky shore. Rudy was puffing on a cigarette, flicking ashes, and smashing them with his foot. I took a dip of snuff and put it between my lips and waited for what I knew was coming.

"Henry," he began, "we been friends for a long time now, but I'm telling you, don't you ever, ever bring him to my place again."

WE WORK IN a different village now, Stephanie and I, up on the slope, an Inupiat village. I have seven years to retirement in this state. It'll be like being set free from prison. I got enough money now, could buy a cabin in the woods, live off the land, eat moose and caribou, salmon all summer during the runs. Sometimes I wonder what the hell I'm doing, an old Montana roughneck like me, teaching second grade. Last summer, back in Montana, I ran into one of my old high school teachers, Mr. Drake, my shop teacher. He quit teaching the year after I graduated, he said, been driving a truck for Coca-Cola ever since.

"You ever miss teaching?" I asked him.

"Henry, not a day in my life. Quitting that racket was the smartest thing I ever done."

That made me think. I'm forty-five years old. All the things I could still do.

I began my life in Alaska commercial fishing, until the

bottom dropped out. Toughest job in the world. Out on the ocean day and night, while Stephanie was teaching in Kodiak. In season, we were seeing each other once a month, if that. Made money, though, more money than I ever had. But no health care, no retirement. I got my degree at Montana Tech, but never thought I'd actually teach. What teacher does? But after a season of rough nights on the sea, the idea of seeing Stephanie every day didn't seem so bad. So I sold the boat, got my certificate from the state, and I've been teaching ever since. Sometimes I still think, though, of nights on the water, beneath the stars, at the mercy of the waves, pulling in my catch. Seven years isn't so long away, but still.

The year before Gary came to Kakarak, at the annual district in-service in King Salmon, Stephanie and I went out to the Oystercatcher, one of my old haunts from those fishing days. A lot of teachers were there. Most of those teachers work in dry villages, and they get to a town like that and they just go nuts. Drunk and Stupid, dancing hand in hand. The bartender, Dennis, was an old friend of mine. Pitchers for Stephanie and me were on the house. A few buddies from my fishing days were in the bar that night, including Matt Sedarsky.

"Man, Henry," he told me, "you got out just in time. The bottom dropped out, the government regs have taken over. Nothing's been the same. Remember? We were pulling in twenty, thirty thousand a season. Now we're lucky just to scrape by."

We were drinking our beers, talking old times. I was feeling good. Meanwhile, other teachers were living large, dancing on tables, grabbing ass, being loud.

Earlier, when I had walked in that night, I passed two teachers—a married couple who'd been in the district awhile, and a third person, a man I didn't recognize. They were all in the parking lot, sitting in the front of an old pickup truck. Never mind about their names—they still teach in that district. Anyway, Hubby sees us, says, "Hey, Henry, Stephanie." I leaned down to look in the car. His wife had a stricken look on her face. I saw between them on the seat, three lines of coke on a flat, small mirror. "Want to join us?" he asked in a high spastic voice.

"Not my thing," I said, and led Stephanie into the bar.

So anyway, later, they were all in the bar. We were sitting at the table, shooting the shit, when Hubby starts dancing like an idiot, shaking his ass. He was wearing these baggy pink pants and he had long hair back then, and a nose ring. He took a bottle of beer, shook it, held it down by his crotch, and opened it, spraying people in the room.

"Knock it off, you jackass," said one of the fishermen at the bar. To that point, I had no dog in the fight. Dennis told Hubby to pipe down, and his wife grabbed his hand and led him to a table. We all shook our heads, and turned back to our conversation. A little later, I saw him playing pool.

Our pitcher was empty, the waitresses were all busy, so I walked to the bar. Hubby walked up to me. "Hey, Honey," he said, really putting on a show. I felt people watching me. I mean, I spent time on the water with some of those guys.

"Get the hell away from me," I said. I turned to order our pitcher. Then I felt Hubby's pool cue between my legs. I turned. Everyone, including my old fishing buddies were watching. I grabbed him by the back of his neck and slammed his head against the front of the bar. I saw his eyes roll to white, and he hit the floor.

"Shit, Henry," said Dennis, as he came from behind the bar with a glass of water, and he threw it in Hubby's face, causing him to regain consciousness. When he did, Dennis kicked him out.

When I returned to our table, I could tell from the look on Stephanie's face that it was time for us to go, too. So we left. Hubby and his wife were sitting on the steps outside the bar.

"Hey, man," he called out to me. "No hard feelings." Dumbass. I just kept walking.

I CAN'T LET it go, that night at Rudy's lodge. Who can absolve me but myself, and I have tried, have rationalized the decision we made. If there are pearly gates, and I believe there are, will I be free to enter them? Technically, we never committed a crime. The night I returned from Rudy's, Stephanie pulled the religious card, telling me that I, who had been raised Catholic, should never have left a man—any man—out there to die, that I had broken God's sixth commandment and I told her that it said not to kill, but said nothing about not stopping death, and doesn't the natural world serve its own kind of justice sometimes? And then, slammed doors, angry words, tears. It was the worst fight we ever had, and I didn't understand until later that what I was fighting was for her to stay by me, and what she was fighting for was a reason not to leave, that what we were both fighting for was love, the only battle ever truly worth fighting, and that night I expected to sleep in the guest bed, but she held me and cried, and it was then that I understood love is greater than sin, not so much that it carries more weight, as on a balancing scale, but that it is like the boundless ocean—soft waves smothering and smoothing stone, relentlessly molding the hardness away.

And yet, I apologize to no one, though I'm sorry for it all. I feel remorse, but no regret, a haunting guilt, but not for Gary's death so much as for the perverse satisfaction I still feel knowing that my single great act of violence in this world came from simply turning a deaf ear to the pleas of a dying man. And who, among those of you who would condemn me for that, do not do the same every day?

THAT TUESDAY, I was in the office, making copies and shooting the breeze with Ilene. Gary was sitting at his desk, working on a computer, when his phone rang. It was an in-house call, I could tell from the ring. He sighed. "Send her down, I guess." Pretty soon, one of the high school girls shuffled in, a scowl on her face. Gary told her to come into his office. Then he shut the door. About five minutes later, the door opened.

"Go back to class," he said, and the girl walked into the hallway. She looked down, embarrassed. Gary was smiling.

He waited and then he walked out into the hall. Ilene's eyes met mine, and then I walked out of the office and discreetly followed Gary. He walked up the stairs to Stephanie's class. In front of the students, I could hear him telling her how to handle her discipline problems, letting her know who's boss.

Calmly, Steph listened without a word, but I knew she was seething. So was I. She's got this thing about fighting her own battles, so I kept my mouth shut. But it was all I could do to not cold-cock him, right there. After school, I hung around the office. Sure enough, in came Stephanie. She walked to Gary's office door.

In an even tempered tone, she said, "Gary, you have my word—if I send you a kid, the kid deserves it. Don't ever do that to me again." Then she walked out of the building and started making her way home, not even waiting for me to give her a ride. From the hall I heard girls giggling. Gary walked out of his office.

"She knows good and well she's not supposed to leave until four," he said. "Some of these teachers think it's my fault they can't handle their classes."

"How many kids has she sent you so far this year?" I asked.

He looked at me as if he hadn't known I was there. "That was the first. Why?"

"No reason," I said. "What did Shawna do?"

"Look Henry, I know you need to support your wife right now. But she overreacted. You know how women can be." He looked at Ilene and smiled.

"What did she do?" I repeated.

"She called Stephanie a bitch. But she said it out of frustration, she's having a rough time at home. Her dad's—"

"That's an automatic suspension, isn't it?" I asked.

"You know these kids—that's the way they talk," he said.

"It is now," I said.

Two days later, I rode up the lake after school, just cruising with my hat off, letting the biting wind hit me in the face. I had my fishing pole, my bait, my auger for the ice. Shawna had been in school both days. Gary didn't suspend her, and every time I looked at him, he walked the other way.

I found a quiet spot on the ice, drilled a hole with the auger. I dropped in my line, felt the cold air against my face. Hoknede Mountain stood across the lake against a clear blue sky. "You need to let this go," Stephanie had told me the night before. I tried to think about anything but Gary. I caught three fish, drank coffee from my thermos, and watched the sun as it settled behind the cool blue horizon.

It was when I returned home that night that Stephanie told me about the fire.

Deanna, she said, had gone up to school to grade papers. After grading several, disgusted with her students' work—they weren't making any progress at all—she stepped outside the back door to smoke a cigarette. She thought she smelled something burning. She walked around the building, and as soon as she turned the corner, saw the black smoke rising from beneath the boiler room door. She called Harold, and he and several other men came and were able to put the fire out.

"Did they say what caused it?" I asked Stephanie.

"They didn't know," she said.

I rode over, knocked on Keith's door. He answered, bags under his eyes, book in his hand. He'd been reading by dim lamp light.

"Let's go," I said.

"Again?" he said.

"It's different this time."

We rode up to school, walked into the boiler room. Gary was there, sweeping ashes into a dustpan. The room was still full of smoke, the carbon smell hanging heavy in the air. The walls were lightly charred, and the generator was down, had been shut off. The fire had been small. Luckily there was little damage.

"How bad?" asked Keith.

"Could have been worse," said Gary. "This stuff's so damn old. I keep telling administration it isn't safe. Probably the wiring in here's all rotted out."

"Lucky thing Deanna smokes," I said.

"Yeah," said Gary. "Lucky. That generator will be out all night, though. Probably better cancel school tomorrow at least."

"Probably better," I said. We helped Gary clean up, and then watched as he rode away.

"Accident?" asked Keith.

"Nope," I said. "This was no accident."

The village of Kakarak, like many in Alaska, didn't have police. Most villages rely on VPSO's—Village Safety Police Officers, but Kakarak didn't even have that. They'd had one earlier that year, a woman from Oklahoma, but she'd ended up in the hospital with a heart condition. That's what passes for law enforcement in Alaska—an untrained Oklahoman with a heart condition. The nearest agency was in Anchorage. About six years before, there was a rape case. We were still waiting for that investigation. I learned a long time ago, in the Alaskan bush, law enforcement's a matter you deal with on your own.

THE NEXT DAY was a Friday, the beginning of March, school had been canceled, and I was all geared to get away, take

Stephanie and head up to Rudy's for the weekend, put Gary and this whole place behind us for a couple of days. But Steph had gone and promised Deanna she'd help plan for the awards banquet. So I invited Keith instead, Keith who'd never ridden a snow-machine in his life. I showed him where the accelerator was, how to brake.

"If you see a moose and it charges," I told him, "don't try to turn and run, just keep going straight as fast as you can. If you try to turn around, the moose will catch you and stomp you. If you hit open water, just gun it. It'll be just like water skiing." He looked at me to see if I was joking, but I wasn't.

The weather called for clear skies, temperatures in the twenties. The days were getting longer. We left late in the afternoon. Keith followed me through the wooded trail, and then onto the frozen lake. In front of us, the setting sun cast an orange glow across the ice. Hoknede Mountain stood pink against a darkening sky.

We arrived at the lodge just as darkness fell. I introduced Keith and Rudy, assured Rudy that Keith was nothing like Gary. We ate a dinner of caribou steaks, mashed potatoes, and sourdough bread. Then we fixed Bloody Marys and Rudy passed out cigars.

About midnight, we heard the approaching noise of a snow-machine. I knew right away. "Shh," I said, and I pulled the curtains shut. Rudy turned off the TV.

"Henry," said Rudy, "so help me…"

Gary rode up the groomed road, parked his snow-machine. From outside, we could hear it, idling just beyond the doorway. Then the footsteps, the knock on the door. We sat quietly. He knocked again, more insistent this time. Then, finally, Gary turned away, and we heard the engine fading into the Alaskan winter night.

The next morning we got up, put our warmest clothes on, and headed up the river. The river bed was frozen solid. Our goal was to hunt caribou and maybe wolves, and to check our traps. We got two red foxes. The day was clear, the chaste, white, snow-covered mountains rising against a mystic blue sky. The roar of our motors was nearly drowned by the silence of the tundra expanse.

That night, when we returned, I skinned the foxes, and gave one of the furs to Keith. I told him that back in Kakarak he could ask Chena Elaine to make him a hat, or some gloves with it.

We made a dinner of cranberry salad and caribou sausage with more sourdough bread. Then we mixed screwdrivers, and sat down to a game of poker. We were interrupted occasionally by voices, breaking over the static on the radio.

Sure enough, just like the night before, at midnight, we heard the approaching motor. Through the window I could see the lights. We continued our game, silently, waiting, listening to the radio static, the ticking of the pendulum clock on the mantle. But Gary didn't stop for long, never even dismounted from his snow-machine. We watched out the window as his red taillights disappeared behind a final spray of snow as he hit the ice-covered lake.

A HALF-HOUR LATER, we were still playing cards, when we heard his voice over the radio.

"Mayday," he said. "Mayday! Anybody read?"

The three of us looked at each other and listened for another voice to heed his call.

"Somebody help!" he said. "Anybody? I hit open water. I'm stranded on the lake, and I'm wet! Mayday!" said Gary.

"I'm out," said Keith. He was watching us both closely.

"I raise you a dollar," said Rudy.

"You're on," I said.

"Mayday." The voice was fading now. "Mayday."

"What d'ya got?" I asked Rudy, and he showed me three queens. I laid down my full house, and calmly took my chips. Then, I reshuffled the deck, dealt the cards.

White Collar

IT WAS WELL past three AM. I had just turned forty and my internal tectonics were slipping to fault. Had lately written bad poetry on client invoices. I wanted to be a poet once. Instead I became what I am. I couldn't sit still, woke at all hours of the night. Wanted to live forever, to hurry and die. I still dreamt of hitchhiking through Europe. There was work that would never get done. People asked, and I said I was fine. I was not. Suicide was not an option. We were over seventy-five thousand in the red when it had begun. This was no fault of hers. You've read "The Tell-Tale Heart." You think you can dismiss your conscience, can hide from it. You cannot.

The smell of exhaust, moist dirt in the air. *How could you do this to us?* she had asked. So. A taking of stock, this was. A spring night, May, the newly blooming tulips, forsythias, dogwoods cut in half by street slash porch lights and shadows as I walked the neighborhood streets. For years, I had been actively seeking distraction. A year ago, I purchased an old saxophone at a thrift shop. Sometimes, I took a baseball bat into the yard, and hit tennis balls toward the development houses being built in the gully below. *How could you? How could you?*

The men came to my office. Asked me questions. I knew the answers. I knew they knew I knew the answers. I lied anyway. It was all very cordial.

How could I? Desire, my friends. Old-fashioned want. What I wanted: a fresh start, to make people proud, to pay off the debts, a better job, to walk briskly up stairs and not have to stop to catch breath, to breathe allergen-free air. Lower blood pressure. Lower cholesterol. Higher sex drive. I wanted to re-connect with her, to be again desire-ravished lovers. I want-ed to become the old couple at the end of the block, working our last days together in our garden. I wanted a do-over. To meet her again, back in that old dusty college auditorium on the western Nebraska plains. To have together a child. Fool-ishly, I thought money could do this. Greed, yes, but what I'm trying to tell you is that greed is not all material. But, this tells you nothing. There is no explanation for what I have done. I thought a return to zero would equal a new start. About this, I was right.

Earlier, as I had lain awake in bed, I thought about a long ago night, driving in the snow. Winter, a ground fog moving in, and a train running beside me, racing side by side through the winter night. I had just come out of the mountains, over the pass across the New Mexico slash Colorado border, and I-25, no traffic, two in the morning, and I wouldn't be home until four, maybe later if the fog didn't clear. Home. That trail-er town, lights over the prison. I *knew* what I wanted once, knew what I believed in. That was long ago, long before this job, before our childless marriage, before I'd even met Mau-reen.

Back to that spring night: By 4:00 AM, I was still wide awake. A sedan had turned onto the street, and I hid in the shadows.

I had a good life. I couldn't see it. I watched the sedan pass, the red taillights. I wondered if I was tough enough for prison. I had no tattoos, yet. Needles made me queasy. I'd fainted at a health center once. I walked the neighborhood streets, trying to convince myself it would all work out fine. I returned home at 5:00 AM. I sat on the couch and drank coffee until 7:00. Maureen was still asleep when I left. I ate a hurried breakfast of peanut butter on stale bread, strawberry yogurt, Girl Scout cookies.

I'd been listening to Zeppelin for two straight weeks in my car. Black Dog. On my drive to work that morning, I turned it up, sang along, laughed like a madman. I approached the interstate exit that led to the office. I should have kept driving, and driving, and driving and driving and driving and driving and driving.

But I knew the gates had closed behind me and all I could do was proceed. I walked into the meeting, on time for a change. The partners turned, and I felt all eyes upon me. The men in their suits were there. When they saw me they nodded, rose to their feet. I surrendered my hands to them.

Glass Fragments on the Shoulder of Highway 375

THE LIGHT WAS starting to show on the horizon, and still we were driving, and I looked at her, my Caroline, asleep in the passenger seat, her makeup now smeared, her brown hair matted down in the back, her cheek resting awkwardly against the window. I could see the slight curve of her neck reflected in the glass. I had not slept for nearly twenty hours, was starting to see flashes of light in the road, but I wouldn't stop until we got to the border, to the treatment center. It hit me, then, that my life on this side was over. Borders. I reached to wake her. No matter what happened, or when, I knew I would never go back. Even behind the unnatural frailty, the slow drainage, the withering away that was observable, she was beautiful, beautiful, and I touched her, still felt the vibrancy from the first day on that carousel.

As children, playing in the pine and spruce wooded mountains that surrounded our family cabin, we were warned, told to stay alert, to make noise. We knew the local stories—of the woman and her baby in the trailer, the bears on the roof, tipping the trailer on to its side. The man, trapped in his outhouse, the breath of the bear coming in huffs from beneath the thin plywood walls. I dream of them still, those bears. And the dreams are never of fear, though sometimes I am running, running through their forests.

In the backyard. as you can see, there is a flagstone patio,

and a garden where she would grow flowers, green chili, jala-
peños, tomatoes (tough to grow in the dry, high altitude climate, but she made it work), potatoes, eggplant and whatever
other vegetables fit the climate. There is a balcony on the back
of the house, and a ladder so that we could climb on to the
roof to gaze at the stars. There are trails leading up into the
nearby mountains. You will be happy here, said the agent. We
were. Happy.

It is a cruel joke of Freudian nature that that which
threatens us most cannot be escaped, so we hide beneath skin
veneers, and hope for the best as we walk our daily lives in the
neighborhoods of temptation. And deep within our sleep at
night, our true selves are revealed to us slowly in sound and
image bites that we never truly fit together—the great unfin-
ished jigsaw puzzle of our human lives.

Consider the sock, that most human of inventions, humankind's first move to distance ourselves from the touch of
the earth, a means of sequestering from the natural world.

Okay, let's say you live alone in an apartment in a strange
city. You don't teach school anymore, because the state has
"misplaced" your certification application. You take a part
time job at a bookstore. The owner has seven cats, who laze
comfortably on the shelves between the books. You hate cats,
are allergic. In addition, the owner is a squat woman with a
penchant toward maroon blouses and black slacks. She wears
turquoise scarves. She has dark black glasses, and refers to you

as *hon*, oftentimes when she's telling you to do things that she could just as easily do herself.

I see her, Caroline, her black shoulder-length hair and the purple-framed sunglasses that matched the flowered print dress. I was nineteen, she was twenty. I see her now, moving up and down, in slow motion, riding the carousel at the Cheyenne Mountain Zoo. There are children laughing, and her hair lifts into the air as she rises and passes where I watch, with my camera, snapping shots of her, her dress in the breeze, her hands grasping the metal bar.

Her final gift was a small bear fetish, small enough to keep in my pocket. Before giving it to me, she held it between her hands and then held them up to her mouth. She blew into her cupped hands. "Now," she said, "wherever you go, a part of me will always be with you."

My parents, too, are both gone. My father. Sunday mornings we used to rise early, drive to the reservoir, a small row boat in tow. By sunrise, we would be casting our lines, sparse words shared between us until the drive home. All that silent reflection led to the conversations I remember most. I remember him in that blue rain jacket, his hair mussed and prematurely gray, as mine is now. He talked of his life in Iowa, the farm where he grew up. He told me how, when he was nineteen, he trained as a fighter. "Never mastered taking the punches," he said, "though it was what I practiced most." I tried to imagine him as a young man in trunks, the sound of the speed bag in the background, dust particles dancing in light, the musty smell of the gym. He said he quit when he woke up one day and couldn't remember the seconds that led up to the punch that dropped him. Both farm life and boxing felt foreign to me then as they do now. His uncle had a shop where he kept the x-ray machine, let my father use it ad nauseum.

I dream, still, of my mother in the afternoon, where I swing from a hammock in the desert sun. And the days pass like clouds in a stormy sky, the sky that I remember from my days as a child growing up in the small prairie town. And the kids I knew played with pennies on the churchyard steps. I watched them from across the street on trips into town with my uncle. I heard their laughter and waited for the invitation to join them that never came.

And on the rides home I would watch the colors blur by—the greens, blues, browns and yellows that made up the only world I knew, and I watched the oil pumps in the fields, their heads like giant grasshoppers swaying up and down.

If I was a ghost on earth, I'd walk on railroad tracks, just to feel that old engine run through me. I'd jump on the caboose at the end and ride it through the West. I'd haunt the men, their suit coats on the seat beside them, their loosened ties, their fancy Scotch, in their sequestered jets above the ground. And I'd jump from the highest buildings just to hear my old voice scream. And I'd make noise in the attic just to wake you from your nightmares. I never craved death until I saw fully the evil of humankind's ways, saw it in the withering of all that I've loved.

The fallout from the Upshot-Knothole bomb test series, for example, led to cancer in many of the children who played in the fallout as if it were snow.

One day, a bohemian woman—torn bell-bottom jeans, fluffy white blouse, braless, yin-yang tattoo on her lower back—the whole bit—comes in asking for obscure poetry, that you know Cat Lady wouldn't have on hand in a million years, so you order it and tell her to return in two days, and when she does you give her the books, won't let her pay—"no, really, take them"—and she automatically—and correctly—assumes ulterior motives.

I thought a lot about you, Caroline, yesterday. I was walking in the morning as I always do, watching the stars melt into the bright light of dawn, and I remembered the way it felt when you kissed me that night in the snow storm, Lynnmarie's car running outside where she waited to take you home, and I wanted you to stay. It had been a long time coming. Your lips were softer than I'd even imagined, gentle, and we kissed some more. I still remember lying in bed that night and imagining you there next to me, but the next day you were gone, back to Las Cruces, and I was destined to stay here forever in the snow, the image of your lips still impressed upon mine the only relief from the January freeze.

They are there, always, the bears, on the periphery of my consciousness, and when I do actually see one, it's a brief glimpse and then it's gone. They come to me in dreams, or through movement at the corners of my eyes, like fleeting spirits, quick flashes of that bouncing gait, the dark rounded back, the hump at the shoulders. In New Hampshire, near the White Mountains, just outside the town of Lincoln, moving swiftly through the concentrated light of a street lamp. On the Alaskan Kenai Peninsula, disappearing into the trees that line the road just as I round a curve. In Colorado, running across a wildflower filled valley. It's as if they have been there, always, hidden at the edges of the nocturnal forest, on the outskirts of my conscious mind. If you look long enough, you will see them, too.

So finally you invite her for coffee, one day while Cat Lady's gone, and you lock the store and leave for an hour, and Bohemian Girl tells you about her boyfriend in LoDo, who she's thinking of leaving, and out of the blue you just ask—no finesse whatsoever—"would you like to have an affair, then" and you're thinking the whole time what a creep you've become.

It doesn't take much for most of us.

The most important issue that is important to me when thinking about a house is that there is plenty of space outside. In other words, it is not my dream to have a big house, but I would like a place that sets alone, preferably in the mountains of either New Mexico or Colorado. It is important to me that I have a place where there are lots of trees in a natural rather than landscaped setting, a place where I can see the stars at night, and there are deer and elk close by.

You'll notice if you look at the sketch that the house I would like to live in is an adobe style house. This is no doubt a result of my years living in New Mexico. I like the simple squared-off design of the house, and I think the adobe style fits into the natural setting where I see myself.

I was very interested to read Sales' characterization of deep ecology and the Gaia hypothesis as *radical.* I recently read James Lovelock's book, and didn't find it at all radical. In fact, the notion of the earth being one living organism seems reasonable, and certainly is nothing new. That Sales included this in the same section of the book as Earth First! raised some questions in my mind. I'm not sure what this says about me, but the Gaia hypothesis seems really quite a fundamental way of looking at inhabiting the world, so I can't help but wonder what it means that such a theory is listed under this section of the book. Are we so far removed from looking at the earth as a living ecology, that even a book with a left environmental leaning categorizes the very idea as radical?

For months after she died, I painted images from long ago dreams, of nymph lovers and courtesans, and all the shared happiness that only dreams can bring. It was on the night of the storm and the shipwreck off the coast that her image first came, her haunting aqua eyes and the emerald cross she held with both hands before her, and together we drank poetry through a straw, my blood flowing in waves and her eyes fluttering to the warmth of the liquid as it passed to her lips. And I knew that she knew, and I felt shame worthy of all those men I so held in disdain.

Later, when the men from the ship had disappeared, I would hear their voices forever in the waves, and I watched in the night for the falling emerald star that I knew would soon fall to the ocean from the sky.

I am not suggesting that my affair caused her death. I'm only saying that sin is sin, all of it, flowing like witchery though the same air as love. The men who knowingly poisoned the soil, the air, the men responsible for her death, for the death of my father, are but men, flawed. I hold them no more malice, but...even good men must be held accountable for the evil of their deeds.

My camp is not far down canyon from El Divisadero, a

small train stop along the Pacifico-Chihuahua railroad that overlooks the Barranca del Cobre, Mexico's Copper Canyon. The American tendency is to compare each of the Sierra Madre canyons to the Grand Canyon, but in reality that is like comparing Lassie to a pack of wolves. All five of the canyons—Urique, Sinfrosa, Batopilas, Copper and Guaynopa—that make up Barranca del Cobre National Park could be easily filled by the Grand. Within these canyons are a handful of small Tarahumara Indian villages, and miles of unexplored and enchanting beauty.

"I love wilderness," I have heard such men say. "For a week every summer I take the family and go camping." This may be a vacation, but what it is not, is a "relationship." It is the difference between a marriage and an annual trip to a house of ill repute. Or, between objectifying nature as "other," and seeing oneself, like a fish in the water, moving through a world of air, inhaling, and exhaling, existing as a *participant* on a moment by moment basis.

I was standing in *Fiction*, imagining the bombs of the next world war when through the stacks I saw her walking outside the window and I moved to the screen, placed my hand on it, felt her shadow as she passed, and even now I think about second chances, hearts in a jar, the bald man with the patch over his eye from the bar I frequented at the time. I placed a book by Somerset Maughm in my bag, and sneaked through a back door, outsmarting security. I followed her, let her lead me across the campus path, like words on a page.

A part of her will always go with me.

"In the psyche," writes Clarissa Pinkola Estes in *Women Who Run with the Wolves*, "the bear can be understood as the ability to regulate one's life, especially one's feeling life.... The bear image teaches that it is possible to maintain a kind of pressure gauge for one's emotional life, and most especially that one can be fierce and generous at the same time."

Fierce and generous at the same time.

I asked a student of mine once, a Tohono O'odham Indian named Johnny what it means to dream of bears.

"It means," he said, "that you have a strong mind." And then he added, "But I'm not sure if it works for white people."

Bohemian Girl giggles, but says "yes" of course, because she thinks you are temporarily interesting. Later, at her apartment, you admire her collection of South American folk instruments, and you lie and say how you once traveled through the rain forest when you were fresh out of college, though the truth is that you went to Ecuador once for a week with a church mission group and had disappointed the minister by sneaking out to the village to drink.

Beneath the old oak tree in the city plaza sits the old man alone. He watches unnoticed as the traffic passes, and thinks of the family that he long ago had, and drinks from the three-peso bottle that he got by begging from the businessmen as they passed. He tried to remember what it felt like to wear a suit, to laugh with friends, to share a meal with a neighbor. It all seems so foreign to him now, this far removed from the life that he'd once taken for granted.

The bottle will rescue him, he swears, though he knows what others would say. If nothing else, it will help him to sleep beneath the big old oak tree in the small city park. And he can dream, until the morning policeman kicks him again awake.

A flower, watched through the eyepiece of time, slowly unfolds itself, and reveals its innermost to the sky above. It gives of its nectar, until it runs dry. Then the petals fall, one by one, and rest on the ground until they dry, and the rain mixes them with the soil.

Could I put them all in a pool, swim through them, those memories, let them mix in the waves—what does it mean to not be invited to your own high school reunion, to not even be thought of, to still be invisible to those classmates of thirty years earlier? A fictional character would drive to their homes, seek them out, ask them to remember him. I remain in love with a woman who would save me from my own impulses, a woman I couldn't save back.

What is most uncanny about this short sample of text are the contextual relationships relative to the environmental history that would follow. Consider, for example, the desert location, and the environmental marginalization of the Western states which continues to this day. (The shipping of nuclear waste to Nevada is but one example. And, don't get me started on Libby, Montana). Also, note the relationship between defense materials and a private oil company. (See Iraq). Finally, "reports of human illness," can perhaps be related to high incidence of cancer, allergies and other modern illness. Like Shelley's *Frankenstein,* Carson's *Silent Spring* takes on even more relevance with time, a matter which will be more fully addressed later.

In a box in your closet, you still have her letters. And on cold desert nights in the winter amidst the whiskey fog, you take and read them and imagine her there, holding you. You look at the words, and an old glimpse surfaces of the young woman she was, her hands moving with a flourish across the page, the words a form of magic, touching, haunting you all these years since.

In the Mountain's Shadow

IRENE'S EXASPERATION HANGS heavy like moss. Moments before, Arthur had heard her footsteps clamber up the stairs until she'd emerged carrying a full laundry basket, stopping long enough to harrumph at him, before making her way down the hall to the back bedroom. He sits back in his blue recliner. Already it's late morning. He has yet to attempt the exercises the therapist gave him. Do the exercises and Irene's exasperation will dissipate, and he will feel better. This he knows. Still he sits in the beige room. The blue divan, which Irene spent months deciding on and still isn't happy with, sits against the west wall. Above it hangs a painting: a red barn beneath thunderclouds. They had purchased the painting shortly after moving into this house nearly fifty years ago, had paid only five dollars for it, the barn reminiscent of their Oklahoma past, the price paid a thrift that remains. Arthur has lately taken to watching TV with the sound off. Silence flows from the lips of the midday newsman.

Flickering maple tree shadows blink against the sliding glass door. Beer steins line the fireplace mantle, though neither he nor Irene drinks. Several years ago, at a German restaurant with their kids, he had pointed to a stein on a shelf and casually stated he liked it. Because he is—he has been told this often—nearly impossible to buy for, the stein collection began. For nearly ten years he'd received them, birthdays, Father's Day and Christmas, until the trend finally faded. Steins hold little interest for him now, and he wonders what it was that drew him to them in the first place.

IRENE WALKS IN from putting away the laundry, sits down on the divan.

"I want to hear this," she says, gesturing at the TV. Arthur reaches for the remote on the table beside him, but it isn't there. This confuses him. He realizes it is snuggled next to his leg in the chair. He takes it, turns on the volume, but by then it's too late. The news anchor has already moved on to the next story. Irene sighs.

"Are you going to do your exercises?" she asks.

"I should," he says.

"That's not an answer," she says. To this, he does not reply. They each sit and stare at the TV screen. The moss thickens.

"I swear," she says and then rises and walks out the sliding glass door, onto the deck, down the steps to the yard. The sound of water in the pipes and he knows she is tending the flowerbed. He wishes it would rain. Theraputty, the dough-like substance the therapist suggested he use to improve his fine motor control, rests on the table beside him. He picks up the canister, opens it. Takes out the putty, squeezes it a few times, puts it back.

IT'S THE DRIVING he misses most. Wherever he goes, Irene must drive him, to his doctor appointments, to…where else? There's really no place left to go.

Since his first stroke nearly two years ago, Arthur has spent his days in this reclining chair, watching the small TV, even though a new larger one, purchased by his children last year for his eightieth birthday, sits downstairs in the rec room. They tell him the picture is amazing. Top of the line. The remote control confuses him. All the buttons. Sometimes, when he turns it on, there is no picture. His grandson, Brandon, has shown him several times the correct combination of buttons to push when this happens. Somewhere, there is a manual. He remembers a time when watching TV was a simple matter of a single on and off switch.

When he does go to the basement, it's to the back bedroom and a different recliner, even more comfortable than the one he sits in now. Down the stairs is a journey with a walker at both ends. It is a slow descent, hand over hand on the railing, Irene gripping his belt loop from behind, as if she could hold him should he fall. Sometimes he imagines it as their fitting end, the two of them fallen together, found later, broken bodies tangled at the bottom of stairs.

THEY MOVED HERE from Tulsa, Oklahoma, where he had worked with a small insurance firm, his first professional job. It was a gray November, 1958, when they arrived in this city, with two kids in tow. Irene talks now about how dark the city had been, how unfriendly the people. But Arthur liked it from the start. This neighborhood was long stretches of vacant lots then, just a handful of houses. What few trees grew were recently-planted saplings. Now the trees stand tall and block the view of the mountain from their living room window. That view had sealed their decision to buy the lot in the first place. Now the lots are all filled, most of the homes on second or third owners, people he doesn't know.

Sometimes Arthur moves mentally through the neighborhood, house by house—starting from the north end of the street—and counts the people who have died. Never does he make it all the way through to the south end. Never, in fact, makes it even to their own house, usually stopping when he gets to the Birkerts' home, two doors away. Dr. Birkerts died not of old age, but of a gas leak in the mountain cabin he owned. A tragedy. Unlike dying from old age, Arthur thinks, which is sad, but not tragic.

Arthur will turn eighty-one in August.

Broken. Since the second stroke: a fall that broke his wrist, surgery on his knee, and a spinal fusion after that. Theraputty, hell.

Things he could do: exercise, walk, read, sit on the patio in the sun, go downstairs, read his email, walk to the mailbox, check his stocks online. Instead he sits, feels the sedentary ache in his muscles, feels the diminishing day. He sleeps little at night. His pants are bunched up where Irene has cinched his belt. Middle age robust gut is lost now, and from his very center he feels himself fading.

"Eighty is the new sixty," his oldest son, Keith, had said the year before, after his birthday dinner. Arthur guesses this was meant to make him feel better. Sort of like the cake from which he couldn't have a second piece on account of his diabetes. They were sitting downstairs watching the new TV, a remake of an old Western, which was supposed to be good. Arthur had not known any of the actors. He didn't see the big deal about the movie, but Keith had assured him it had won all the big awards.

"Eighty doesn't feel like any damn sixty," Arthur had said. His ankle ached, and he felt agitated. He realized he'd been tapping his foot again. "Trust me. I know what sixty feels like.

Eighty feels exactly what it is."

"Things could be worse," said Keith. Indeed, Arthur thought, things could.

Recently, Irene told him she'd read the average life expectancy in the United States was seventy-five.

"You are five years beyond average," she said.

Well, he thought. Whoopty damn do.

Irene is not easy to deal with. Arthur knows this. At the hospital, as he lay in recovery from the surgery, he could feel the nurses stiffen when they entered the room and saw her sitting with him. She did not trust the doctors, did not trust their medicine, questioned them every step of the way. He imagined nurses arguing over whose turn to treat him, who would be the one to have to deal with her.

THE NOT-DOING OF exercises has become Arthur's habit. He doesn't know why. He wants to get better. He misses the office. Nights lately, he tosses and turns. He can't sit up without Irene's help. Twice in two weeks, even with the walker, he has fallen trying to walk to the bathroom. He cannot get comfortable in the bed. They have tried three different mattresses. Often, he sleeps in the afternoon, in the recliner. Sometimes he wakes to a wave of guilt. He thinks of his children's divorces. He thinks: *if I'd been a better father if I'd been around more if I'd taken them on vacations....* Divorce. If his mind wanders near Judy Sanderson, he tries to force her image away. The hell of aging: what once was fading memory now returns in vivid recollection.

Back when the mountain and the house and the city were all new to him, Arthur would sit in the living room and look up at Pikes Peak through the large plate window. He would take note of the changing seasons as they turned the mountain from snowcapped white to purple and then back again. Home after a long work day, he would take peace from its silhouetted form standing against the darkening sky. At some point, he can't remember when, a light was placed at the top, along with the new buildings that greeted the old cog railway. At the time, that light felt like a calling beacon. But he had never climbed to it. All these years, and he'd only been there once, by way of the cog rail that had been built to take tourists to the top. He remembers Keith playing in a pile of snow. Remembers the small cramped gift shop, and kitschy hoopla about the donuts, how they fry up bigger at 14,000 feet, or some such thing. It seemed oddly American to him: all that thin air, views that stretched out beyond the city below, and the top draw of the summit a silly donut. When they had first moved here, he'd been determined to climb the peak one day. It was a common thing for people to do. All four of the kids had climbed it at least once; Daniel had even run the marathon to the top one year. But Arthur had never even started up the trail. What had he done instead? He had worked, mostly. Worked, gone to his kids' ballgames, their student-teacher conferences, their recitals, their graduations, their weddings, their baptisms. In the years since his children had moved on, he had watched a lot of TV, had been to a handful of Rotary dinners. He can think of little else. More than once he has been told he needs a hobby. Springs like this, he used to work in their garden. At first, when he could do that no longer, he yearned for it. Now, he can't see what pleasure he would find in it at all.

The house they live in is silent most of the time. Once it

was filled with a toyland of chaos. They have, all of them, been very fortunate. A functional family. Rare enough these days. He thinks back with a sense of bewilderment how close he had once come to losing it, to throwing it all away.

THE LAST TIME he was in the hospital was supposed to be overnight, and just for a series of tests. He ended up staying five weeks; it was finally determined he needed the spinal fusion surgery. The knee was still in recovery, was taking longer than they had hoped. It was explained to him: surgery comes with risks, especially at his age. Well no kidding, he thought. He remembered back, his father, the shock of the doctor's words, his mother sobbing in the corridor.

The spinal fusion surgery, though, had gone well enough. "You should feel fortunate," the surgeon had said.

Fortunate. Five years over the average. His father had died at sixty-seven; his mother in a nursing home at ninety-one. When he goes to the physical therapist, Arthur's prescribed exercises include using an elastic stretch band for his wrist and walking on a treadmill for his knees. Each time he steps on that treadmill feels like a race that he's losing.

In addition to Keith and Daniel, Arthur and Irene have two daughters, Paula and Kathleen. They each have lives of their own, the usual problems and successes. Divorces, debt, children with ADD. Decent jobs, homes in good neighborhoods. Who knows what else? There is much, he is sure, they don't tell him. He imagines what secrets they might hold, what debts, what heartbreak. It is the divorces—Keith, seven years now, and Paula who has been re-married for six—that bother him most. A lot of things bother him. He sees in his grandchildren a disturbing shallowness, a lack of pride. His oldest grandson, now nineteen, has never held a job from what he can tell. Sloppy dresser, always fiddling with his cell phone, even as Arthur is talking to him.

"It's a different world," Irene tells him. It's her answer for everything grandchildren-wise.

"Not that different," he says. "There are nineteen-year-olds working all over the place, if you look around." But he isn't even sure that it's true. Seems to him people don't value work like they once did. In the youth of today he sees ghostly shells of the country he once knew.

They have not seen Paula, their daughter, for two weeks now, and Arthur suspects he knows why. Paula, who teaches 4th grade, had come for dinner on a Saturday night with her second husband, Gerald, the school district union representative. When Paula had first introduced them, several years ago, Arthur assumed she was dating Gerald just to spite him. As it turned out, though, despite his union involvement, Gerald was tolerable. Not entirely un-hateable—that god-awful hippie pony tail, for example—but certainly not so bad as Arthur suspected he'd be. In fact, despite his early reservations, Arthur had grown fond of Gerald. For one, he worked hard. He had served in the Army, had been to Vietnam. Most of all, from what Arthur could tell, Gerald treated Paula well, unlike her first husband, who had impregnated her out of wedlock and then left her when the child, Timmy, was just a toddler. Irene says he had been abusive, but Arthur is unconvinced. Arthur is philosophically opposed to divorce, but was embarrassed to discover relief when it had finally happened. Irene, however, was crestfallen, and had never really forgiven Paula, not for the pregnancy, not for the divorce. Sometimes, Arthur believes, Irene has unrealistic standards for them all.

One fall, several years before, Irene and Daniel had argued. It was after Daniel had first graduated from Western State, hadn't found employment yet. His plan was to move to New Orleans, work odd jobs, "bum around the country" as he put it. Arthur knew it was a harebrained idea that would pass soon enough. With Daniel, Arthur had learned, though good sense was a train that arrived late, it would ultimately arrive. Daniel required patience. Patience was not Irene's strong point. Unpleasant words had been volleyed. What words, Arthur couldn't say. He had left the room.

Later that night, he and Daniel sat out on the patio in lawn chairs. A clear night, a quarter moon making shadows out of branches.

"You know, Dad," Daniel had said. "It doesn't really matter what any of us do. Disappointment is her default mode." Arthur has never forgotten that. He remembers the early years of their marriage, arriving home to her and the children after work, how the life they were building together had filled her with, if not joy, a sense of satisfaction. It occurred to him that the default mode Daniel referred to might be the result of a betrayal she had never seen coming.

So. That dinner two weeks ago. It was just the four of them. Arthur, Irene, Paula and Gerald. There had been discussion about some school board members who were forcefully campaigning for school vouchers. One of them, it turned out, had been an anti-union advocate in San Diego, and was threatening layoffs. Local news filled with reports of contentious board meetings, accusations among the members themselves. For

Arthur, it was all a topic better left un-broached at a Saturday night dinner. But broached it had been.

"How many bad teachers are there, that can't be fired because of the unions?" Irene had said. "Too many."

"Mom," said Paula, "you don't know. You don't work in schools, you don't have kids in schools. Can we just drop it, please?"

"I pay taxes," she said.

"You do realize we are number forty-seven in the nation on education spending."

"Yes. It's always about more money, more money. But never about doing away with the waste."

Arthur was glancing at Gerald who was calmly helping himself to more mashed potatoes. He'd heard it all before.

"It *is* about money. At Timmy's high school, they don't even have enough lockers it's so overcrowded."

"Timmy's problem," said Irene, "has nothing to do with the money spent in schools."

"What's that supposed to mean?" asked Paula.

Oh, tread lightly for once, Irene, thought Arthur.

"I think it's hard on kids, divorce. To be split between two homes like this."

"It is hard, Mom," said Paula. "A lot of things are hard." There was a time when such words would have escalated. Silverware thrown. Rising voices. But Paula had just gone quiet, seething. And then Gerald had turned to Arthur and asked him about an investment. Thought it might be an opportunity worth considering. Arthur had not thought it sensible at all, but was glad for the digression. The conversation turned. Things seemed fine. But Paula and Gerald had left immediately after the meal, and haven't been heard from since.

Yesterday, Sunday, they had spent the day alone, just the two of them. Arthur and Irene. Not one of the kids had called. Sunday night was the time they all used to call. He spent most of the day slumped in his chair.

"Are you okay?" Irene asked.

"Yes," he'd said, because he didn't have the words for it. Monday he would face another week of no place outside the confines of house to go.

FOR THE PAST several years, on Mondays and Wednesdays and sometimes on Thursdays, Arthur worked in an office in a building he once owned. The deal he'd made with McFadden, Murphy and Gorman when he'd sold the business was that he would work with them for three years, an agreement for which he was paid both salary and a percentage of all profits. Also, over the course of the three years, he would phase into retirement. That was the original agreement. Thirteen years later, though, he was still showing up at the office, still working his old accounts. He had simply refused to retire. And so his contract had been annually extended. Graciously, he supposes. Deep down he had known they no longer needed him, but he still did the work and the clients—the few he had remaining—kept coming back. A good man, they said. Honest. Decent.

He should have seen it coming, but wasn't prepared when the three partners took him to lunch and told him it was time to retire for good. This was shortly after he'd finally returned to the office after the last surgery. The day before that lunch, the secretary, Stacia, had found him slumped face down on his desk. She had screamed, and when he awoke, he looked up to several people standing in his doorway, staring. Already, he realized, he was a ghost in their eyes.

Home is a reminder of all he's become—a decrepit old man who needs to be taken care of. "You have to take care of yourself," he'd been hearing for years, from his doctor, his kids, but mostly Irene. Pleading has evolved to scolding. "Put those back, Arthur," she says when he takes candy from the jar on the living room table. "Arthur, we're going to be eating dinner in 20 minutes," she says with disgust whenever he pulls slices of bologna from the refrigerator. "Arthur, have you done your exercises today?" she asks, even when she well knows he hasn't.

The refuge of work now taken away, he can feel his mind slipping.

"I need to go the store," Irene would ask him. "Do you want to go with me?"

And he would not answer. It was not that he couldn't hear. It was that he couldn't decide.

For a brief time, in the early seventies, Arthur had imagined Pikes Peak as a manifestation of God, imagined Him looking down with shame. It was a time even now that he can make no sense of, a time, when he looks back on it, that feels most like a film, watched from afar. He doesn't know how to frame it, why it haunts him. It was shortly after his father died. Death was a new reality. Arthur had always been the responsible one: family man, a good student, the oldest son.

One day, a couple weeks after his father's funeral, Arthur took a long lunch, something he rarely did, and drove aimlessly through the city. He drove downtown, past Thompson's

Sporting Goods, past Klein's clothing, past Theresa's, the ice cream shop. It was a sunny winter day, warm enough to drive with a window down. He turned the radio to a Top-40 station. "Your Mama Don't Dance, Your Father Don't Rock and Roll." He'd heard the song a million times, had heard his own children sing it. He realized how accurate it was. We don't dance, don't rock, don't play ball, don't climb mountains, don't travel, don't ski, don't make love anymore. He had moved to Colorado with the idea that it would be a place of, if not adventure, then…what? He felt an uncharacteristic restlessness. He drove past Acacia Park, which, in the middle of the afternoon on a workday, was full of people. Young people. The women, even beneath their winter coats, wore short skirts. The men had long hair. They all wore casual clothes, bright colors. Two black men with Afros sat on a bench nearby. One of them wore a cowboy hat with a feather in it. They were laughing. Many of the kids were smoking cigarettes or who knew what else. There was a sexual energy to everything, a lack of the restraint he had known in his own life. A new coyness flitted around the edges of women, he'd noticed, even the ones who worked at the office. Every smile seemed an invitation. A song came on the radio. Part of the song had a child singing about a shiny new nickel.…he sat and watched the people in the park. He felt the hair rise on his arms. The world became blurry. It was the first time he had cried since his father died.

IRENE COMES IN from the yard, now. Looks at him, still sitting in his chair. Shakes her head, lets out a deep sigh.

"What?" he asks.

"Nothing," she says. She walks into the kitchen, begins to

make lunch. No longer does he feel hunger, just an understanding he needs to eat. Where once food held pleasure, now each meal feels like a test with the final score a number on his blood glucose machine. He feels tired, wants to sleep. Tomorrow, he will go to the office, he thinks. But then remembers, and there is a slow tightening in his gut. Maybe he will go anyway, just drop in to say hi. But he knows he would only be treated with congenial tolerance, and faced with sly glances at watches.

Irene and his children think he must be going deaf. But he can hear just fine. He doesn't know why he keeps the TV sound off, really. He mostly watches news. Sometimes a crime drama. He can usually figure out the gist of it all without hearing the voices. Most news is not new. It seems to him he once spent most of his life believing others smarter than him, more worldly, better read. But—and he remembers the exact moment—one day he realized that everyone else was just as confused as he was, that most of what he heard he'd heard before, that what he'd so long thought of as smart was merely mimicry. He hasn't heard a fresh idea or story in ages. If Arthur had to describe them, he would say he and Irene are middle-America, church-going Republicans. Some days, though, he watches the news and considers the possibility that everything he's ever believed in is wrong.

"No one knows how to be honest anymore," Irene says. It's one of her catch phrases. And each time she says it, he cringes, wonders if those words are meant for him.

The line between decent and flawed. Crossed so easily. Lust disguises itself as healthy desire.

That day. He had not wanted those laughing men to see his tears. There was a street south of downtown known for prostitutes and drugs—a growing phenomenon that was new then, more frightening. The country had come out of the sixties with a new sense of freedom, but also a hangover specter of lost soul. Sin seemed a reasonable response. He drove up and down that street. He thought about Korea, about Japan.

By the time he returned to work, his whole body was shaking.

The first time, weeks later. A business trip in Los Angeles. A hotel bar. The woman was younger, wore bell bottoms and a long-sleeved T-shirt. Each song on the juke box seemed to speak only to him. "Killing Me Softly," "Me and Mrs. Jones," For a little over a year, after that, there had been a string of infidelities, a directory even now he can replay in his mind, culminating in Judy, the receptionist at the office of one of his clients. A fling at first, and then an obsessive love that found him taking long lunches, leaving work early. Now, as he looks back on it, he is embarrassed at how easy the lying had been, how well he had hidden their secret. Sex lurks easily behind hotel curtains. But love is a hard emotion to mask. Judy became a decision to be made.

In the seventies, he remembers, it had not been uncommon for men he knew to leave their wives for younger women. Many of the men he once worked with had done so. Through his clients, his friends, he had seen the pain it had caused. He and Irene had four children. Judy and her husband had two. They had talked it out the two of them, Arthur and Judy. He played it in his mind and liked it, the very sound of her name next to his. Still, he felt a loyalty if not to Irene than to their children. Did he love her still? He would waver. Sometimes, he would tell Judy he could not see her anymore.

She would cry, and he would end it. For good. And then, two days later, one of them would call the other, and it would begin all over again.

One night they drove through an older part of the city, looked at houses. Judy in the passenger seat, a streetlight and shadow cutting her face in half. He thought she was the most beautiful woman he had ever seen. Could he have afforded two houses? He knows that answer now. Yes. He could have.

THE STROKE ITSELF, the big one, the first one, had struck on a Sunday. He remembers because they had not gone to church, which they almost always did. He had simply not wanted to go, had felt tired. And he was angry, besides, since, several months earlier, the new choir director had encouraged Irene to quit singing with them. "The voice changes with age," the director had explained. Irene, uncharacteristically, had gone down without a fight. She had been a music major, had taught music, had sung in that choir, had played the piano, even filled in on the organ once in a while when the regular organist was gone. She had sung solos in that church. Had even sung in the city chorus for a time.

Arthur was surprised at his own anger. "We've been members of that church for fifty years," he reminded her. "I've been a deacon, we tithe. How *dare* he."

"Arthur, we don't give money so that I can sing," she said. "Besides, it's true. My voice shakes when I sing, I can hear it. He's right."

"Your voice is fine," he said.

"Arthur, drop it," she said, so he had. But he could see how, for a time, it had depressed her. She had stopped playing piano in the afternoons, had stopped listening to the classical radio station.

So, it was a Sunday, and he'd been downstairs, with the TV on, and there was a choir singing the "Hallelujah Chorus" on the TV and he knew Irene would want to hear it. He called to her, though he knew she probably wouldn't hear him. He stood up, took two steps, and fell. It was not the first time he'd fallen. But this time, when he tried to get up, he could not. He felt his heart pounding. His whole body shook. By the time Irene came down, several minutes later, he was still lying on the floor.

"What are you doing down there?" she asked.

"I fell. Can't get up," he said. He noticed then, the slur of his words. She tried to help him, but it was no use.

"I'm going to call 9-1-1," she said.

"No you're not," he said. "Just give me a minute."

"Yes I am," she said.

Soon, the paramedics were in his house, helping him sit up, asking him questions. He remembers feeling no pain, something that confused him. If you fall, and can't get up, it seemed to him that you should feel more hurt. He remembers that his left side was numb, that when he'd put his hand down to push himself up, he hadn't been able to feel the floor. And then he was in an ambulance and a hospital, where he stayed for two weeks. The CAT scan confirmed what he'd already suspected.

"I told you we should have gone to church," Irene joked with him later. He imagines if the fall had happened in the sanctuary; he can think of nothing worse. He was happy they'd been home, hoped none of the neighbors had seen the ambulance in their driveway.

•

IN HIS BLUE chair, he wakes from a nap, hears a plane overhead. He pulls the arm of the recliner, and with the grind of
the springs, he is set upright. He reaches for his walker, strug-
gles to stand. Leans forward once and tries to rise, but loses
his balance and is back in the chair, tries again, only this time
Irene is there, holding the walker steady, lifting him by the
arm. Up now, he moves to the living room, leans on his walker and looks out at the mountain, which is still covered with
snow. A vengeful God, that mountain. He remembers thinking so. During his affair with Judy. On his drive, after a late
afternoon with her, he would feel a wrathful shadow upon
him. At home he would be greeted by his children, would
patiently answer their questions. He was amazed at how
easy it was, how private his secret life. It was then he realized
how unoriginal the world could be. The world was one long
drawn-out story repeating itself over and over. His infidelity
was not the new plot it felt. But wasn't all love like this, fresh
only to those who inhabited it? His was an old story, a para-
ble, a cautionary tale. Were other men doing this? Of course
they were. Women, too. Irene? He doubted it, but so what if
she was. It would only vindicate him. Had he fallen out of
love with her? He was never sure. Was he ever really in love
with her? He would smoke cigarettes in the old hotel room
with Judy, and try to remember what he'd first felt when he'd
met Irene. Sometimes during the time of that affair, he would
make love with Irene. And when he did he would think of
Judy, and wonder whom he was cheating on most.

Once, Judy had flown to Tucson with him on one of his
work trips. Her marriage was already ending by then. He

supposes he was at least partly to blame, though Judy swore to him he had nothing to do with it, that her husband knew nothing about him. It was a difficult weekend. When he called Irene from the hotel phone, Judy sat beside him, and the conflation of it all—Irene's voice on the line, Judy's body beside him—felt more like betrayal than sex ever had. For the first time since he'd started seeing her, Arthur wished Judy would leave. They fought, and Judy left the room. When Arthur found her later, she was in the hotel bar talking to a salesman from Seattle.

The flight home the next day was a rough ride through turbulent skies. Harrowing, filled with stomach-rising jolts. The woman sitting beside him—he and Judy had been careful not to get seats together—cried in fear. Arthur remembers thinking that he alone, was responsible for that turbulence, and as he looked over at the gray faces of the other passengers, he thought about how far-reaching and subtle were the effects of his sin, how easily one could convince themselves that there would never be repercussions, until one day it all came crashing down.

When the plane landed, he had looked up at the mountain, and felt the wrath of its shadow.

So lost in his own secrets, time spent at work making up for the time spent away from it, time at home exhausted, sitting in front of the TV watching the children play. So exhausted, and so lost in his world, that he did not see the crash happening before him. It was not until later—sitting with Irene at the hospital, holding her hand as the doctor described her condition as a nervous breakdown—that guilt finally came over him. She had refused the doctor's pills. Pills mask pain. She had wanted her pain to be evident.

Like every other aspect to his life, he had been meticulous, careful. Never without a prepared excuse. How she knew, he never understood. The following year, after the affair had ended, trying to mask the tremor he felt, Arthur had introduced Irene to Judy at a Rotary dinner. Irene had looked Judy in the eye, smiled sadly, and then had simply turned and walked away. She left him at the dinner alone to explain away her absence as illness. When he arrived home later, she was not there, and he had paced, frantically waiting, unsure how long to wait before making calls. Just after one o'clock in the morning, he was shaking, holding the phone in his hand, when he heard the doorknob turn, and she walked inside. She looked him directly in the eye, said, "Were it not for my children, I would have walked away forever." Later, he determined she had walked nearly seven miles, through poor neighborhoods, through dark sections of town. That night a wide canyon ran down the middle of their bed, and he felt all of its depth as he lay awake and imagined the sound of her footsteps as she walked beneath street lamps, imagined all that might have happened to her.

HE COULD NEVER have imagined it, the loss of control: of his body, his legs, his bowels. Could never have understood "need" as something so basic. Everyone knows the peril of aging. He had seen it of course, in his own mother, in Irene's folks. But you cannot imagine it, cannot know the true horror of it, until you've lived it. He thinks of Dr. Birkerts, of a gas leak death in sleep. He and Irene have no garage. He wonders if he'd go through with it if they did.

One day a week, he used to join his friends for coffee at the donut house at the end of the block. Old men discussing their ailments, their children, the values of a world that no longer existed. Grandchildren. Bad knees, bad backs, bad livers, bad spines, bad memories, bad hearing, cataracts. Heart surgery, skin cancer, hip surgeries, knee surgeries. Friends who have died. The last time he joined them, he sat and didn't talk at all. Bill Simpson had gone on for twenty minutes about his gout. Arthur couldn't think of a thing to say. There was a time he could make people laugh. Now his wit was worse than his knees. The week before, he had tried to repeat a joke he'd heard on TV, only he couldn't get it right, couldn't remember the punch line. He hadn't been back to the donut house since he lost his job.

Each day, when Arthur was in the hospital, Irene had come to stay with him, to sit in the small room and listen to the doctors and nurses, the talk about his diet, his therapy plan.

Irene, Irene. Does she resent him again, as she surely must have once? Her whole life has been spent caretaking—her children, him, the elderly at the nursing home where she volunteers, the souls of those she loves and prays for. She seems to him now, in her role as his caretaker, regal, more beautiful in age than she had been in youth—her hair not yet fully gray, her faith still strong, her love for him intact despite it all. Or was it just loyalty? Was it one and the same? Their children, now with children of their own, perhaps soon would begin to appreciate the prickly obstinacy they once saw as overly strict, to see it for the discipline it was. Even Paula, on a good day Arthur believes, understands her mother's criticism as love.

And it was *she* who raised them, he realized, even in the darkest days of her breakdown, it was always the children she had in her best interests. Not leaving him, as well she could have, was for them, and so she had sacrificed her own desires, her own vision of their life together for them, a vision she must have felt a delusion as she lay heartbroken in her hospital bed, as she walked home through the city that night years ago.

He wonders sometimes, even now, if she might still leave him. If he might wake up one morning, unable to lift himself out of bed, unable to dress, only to find her gone, and a note with a single word: "Ha."

ONE NIGHT, JUST weeks ago, they had gone out to dinner. He had been feeling okay; it was the first night they'd been out for a while. Daniel was visiting for the weekend with his wife, Carla. They went to a restaurant they'd once frequented, but hadn't been for years, a steakhouse. Daniel talked about his job with a resigned joy, a style Arthur recognized as his own. He watched Carla and Irene, how easily they talked to one another.

When the waiter came, though, he didn't know what to order. A simple everyday matter, ordering a meal at a restaurant. But he froze. There were foods he could have, foods he couldn't, the steak was fine, but he wasn't sure about the potatoes, and he sat, silent, could feel the blood rush to his face. Or was the steak fine? There was fish, which he knew was okay, but he couldn't think, couldn't decide. In the end, Irene had tried to order for him.

"Let me do it," he said, louder than he'd intended. He felt Carla glancing up at the waiter, smiling, embarrassed. He looked down at the menu, picking at random and ending up with a salmon fillet and asparagus, a vegetable he hated.

Later, on Sunday, after Daniel and Carla had left, he sat out on the patio, in an old lawn chair he realized needed repair. The lawn needed fertilizer, the house needed painting. His breathing felt labored. Earlier at dinner, his hand had shaken so hard it caused him to spill his water when he tried to drink from his glass. The television screen earlier had flickered, the images freeze-framing and then going dark. Had it an antenna, he could fix it. But he didn't even know what a satellite was, much less how it worked. Daniel had remarked earlier about the computer downstairs, how slow it was, that maybe it was time for a new one.

"It's only five years old," Arthur said, exasperated.

"That's old in computer years," said Carla.

Decay. Damned inevitable decay. It is all around him. Even in the new, in the young. He can look down the street and see it: the lawns going brown, cracked bricks in the foundation of the Hollingsworth's house across the street, potholes in the pavement. Recently, as a cost cutting measure, the city had turned off the streetlights in the neighborhood. An old pickup further down is rusted, the blue painting cracked around the fender. The faded wood fence where the Birkerts once lived leans, some of the pickets missing. There are no children in this neighborhood, he realizes, and few people have pets anymore. The whole neighborhood is haunted by what it once was, and what remains is a testament to the inevitability of decay. Decay in the houses, decay in the people who live in them, decay in the trees, many of which seem to be suffering through blight and rot. It has not rained in ages.

Earlier that afternoon, the clouds had come, covering the mountain, growing dark. Thunder. Part of the decay is in the perpetual dryness, and he longs for a rain that never comes. Optimism, he realizes, mimics those afternoon storm clouds. A promise of cleansing rain, of reprieve from relentless day. It is a glimmer of hope that never materializes. By late afternoon those clouds are gone, the empty flower beds still parched, barren. Joyless.

What is joy anyway? In his 80 years—that was 29,200 days or over 700,000 hours—how much was filled with joy? Or, forget joy. Meaning, even? How many of those hours really mattered? Make every moment count, the saying went. But when he thinks back, the moments that mattered were few. If he were to think hard on it, he supposes he could come up with a list of maybe one hundred. Maybe one hundred brief glimpses of joyous memory in the fog of all those days and hours, and many of those couched in a sin that he fears in the end will define him. It is his biggest fear; that in his death, Irene will reveal his secret to them all.

EVENING NOW AND he sits on their front patio, leans on the walker in front of him. The sky is clear. A woman he doesn't recognize walks her dog on the sidewalk. She wears a knit hat, red with orange stripes. He wonders if she has made it herself. Do people still do that? Knit their own hats? She greets him as she passes, smiles. She is young. Of course, everyone is young to him now. He wonders if she is married. Behind the mountain rests blue sky, the same sky he remembers from the first time he came here, the sky that convinced him to move here in the first place. He wonders what Irene is doing, wishes she'd come sit beside him. He places his leg in front of him, stretches. Maybe by spring he will walk all the way to the corner. If he starts doing his exercises.

The air is cool. A diabetic cold in his feet; he knows he should go inside. He wants to dissolve this idea of decay. He tries to think of the two of them, Arthur and Irene, when they first came to Colorado. His mind slips and he thinks instead of Judy. He remembers her, after they had made love, lying naked on top of the hotel bedspread. He wishes he could see her again. Wishes he could be there again in that hotel room. Where would they be now, the two of them, had he made the decision to leave Irene? The men he knew who left their wives for someone else: over the years, he has encountered these new couples, and even when the women were considerably younger than their husbands, they had all seemed to age so quickly. It puzzles him. He can't see, not in one case, where the men had been better off. And yet, always he has wondered. Would the inevitable decay have begun for him sooner? He loved them both, in different ways, but even now he does not know if the love he felt for Judy was a real or a deluded justification. How easily the mind can fool. He imagines people watching Irene help him into the car, take his walker and place it in the backseat. Real love, they must think, and it is. It is not only the dishonesty of the infidelity he has carried as a burden; it is the ease with which he once lied to himself, that by defying the standards of fidelity, he had believed, foolishly, that he could also defy the decay.

Judy, he knows, died several years ago. He had seen it in the paper. He had not sent flowers, had not mourned, had not, of course, mentioned it to Irene. He had simply read the obituary, had a brief flutter of melancholy, and turned the page. He feels shame at it now, but remembers too that he had felt something else: relief. It is a sense not uncommonly felt when people die, he is sure of it, something that nobody ever admits. He wants to tell Irene that it will be okay to feel that way, too.

He hears the screen door open and close, hears her footsteps on the carport.

"Do you want to come inside?" she asks. With one hand she holds his walker steady while she places her other under his arm and lifts him to a stand.

She could have walked away forever. Instead she is here. Tonight, he will lie awake beside her, listen to her sleep. In the morning, light will show on the tip of Pikes Peak and slowly descend toward them. She will help him sit up on the bed, will pull his socks over his swollen feet. She will bring his walker, help him stand, help him into his pants, zip them, help him run a belt through the loops and buckle it. She will walk behind him, help him to his blue recliner, where he will sit and stare into the cold glow of the TV's silence.

Anniversary

HE FEELS THE creaking in his aged knees as he ascends the steps onto the porch upon his return from a walk that had found him, despite the autumn rain, passing the beachside park where his habit had long been to turn around, but instead, today he had walked into the town on the other side of the bay across from the lighthouse his family had tended since it was built in 1886, the lighthouse where still he lives, alone now, and he had considered stopping at the Bayside Bar when he passed, but there would be no one he knew, since Bernie, the old bartender and Ed and Cecil, his drinking buddies had all long since passed away and besides, he was in no mood for company, better to drink alone for an old man like me, he thought, especially on this night, the night that marked his 60th wedding anniversary, or would have, had Edith not died in the spring, a torture he tried to subdue by concentrating on the sound of fallen leaves crunching beneath his feet and the distant Lake Superior waves crashing against the rocky coast, but it was no use, her death was all around him, and—like his declining vision, arthritic bones, embarrassment of failing memory and bladder—inescapable; so he trudged his way through town and into the neighborhoods he once knew so well but now seemed foreign, as he did not recognize the people he passed on the street, the children playing football in yards, the new cars parked in the driveways, and he was struck again with the weighty agony that his friends and family were all dead and he carried this with him back to the only home he had ever known, the empty lighthouse that was built to save lives of sailors lost in fog but now only carried a small plaque—like a grave marker—that recognized the lighthouse as a National Historic Landmark, and now he stands on the porch looking out over the lake, fog moving in and he takes the key in his shaking hands, turns it in the lock, opens the door, takes off his coat and hat, neatly hanging them in the closet, blows warmth into his stiff hands, walks into the living room to turn up the furnace, then back in the kitchen where he opens the cupboard above the sink, pulls out the old bottle that had been given them many years before by the Coast Guard at a dinner banquet to honor the tending of that light that beaconed boats away from dangerous cliffs, and he wipes the dust from the bottle, remembers the story of its discovery by Lake Superior divers investigating a shipwreck and it was then at least seventy years old, and it survived—where so many sailors had not—without so much as a chip in the thick glass of the bottle, and he curses the fact he will drink it alone after all those years they had talked about one day sharing its mystery on a special occasion that only the two of them would understand, but for all those years it sat on the shelf, and though he isn't sure what, something draws him to the bottle now, and he takes out a corkscrew, drives it deep into cork, feels the ache in his joints, his fingers, his wrist as he pulls with what little strength he has left, until, finally, with a loud pop that causes him to stagger, the bottle comes uncorked and he carries it into the living room, slumps into his E-Z chair, pours a drink, takes a sip, leans back, closes his eyes, *to you*, he says, tips the glass toward the ceiling, takes another sip and it is thick like syrup and strong, unlike any drink he has ever known, and he feels a draft, but, oddly, it does not feel cool, but warm, and he turns to look at the door which he has indeed closed tightly—*must be the fireplace vent*—and he sits back in his chair, lets the effects of the drink fill him, allows the memories, the ones that he has been suppressing all day, and he thinks of her, the life they had, that summer in '48, when they met at a bazaar in Marquette where he helped his father, who besides tending lighthouse was a portrait photographer, and she was working at the bake sale where he bought three pies and a cake before finally gathering courage to talk to her, and a year later they were married and on a honeymoon in Chicago, having taken the train, a first for them both, and that night in the old hotel in the dark neighborhood, the one with the paint chipping off the walls, the water that only ran cold, the heater that was stuck, making the room so hot that he had slumped onto the bed, dripping with sweat, frustrated and embarrassed, had wanted so badly to impress her, but she simply opened the window and sidled next to him, whispered, it's *all right*, and the sweating continued into the morning and for the next fifty-nine years she amazed him time and again the way she could take a small catastrophe and make it something good, until that day they lost their one and only, the child Abigail, in the fire, and Edith had lived her remaining days never far from the grief, never, he knew, fully forgiving him for the loss, and finally they moved back into the lighthouse after his parents passed away, where he tended it full time upon his retirement from the packing company, and then, when the lighthouse closed, he was allowed to stay on as primary caretaker, so that when she retired, they had spent evenings in solitude watching liners pass on their way to the Locks at Sault Ste. Marie, weathering the many winter storms that rose from the lake, listened to jazz records on the old phonograph and he continues to drink as the memories flow, and again he feels the draft, but when he rises to check, the fireplace vent is closed, the fireplace, that fire, that damned night that haunts him, haunts him, and he hears a noise from outside, tires, a car pulling into the driveway, he thinks, but when he peers out his window, all he sees is the empty gravel road covered with leaves and the near-barren trees that line it and as he stands quiet and listens, he hears the waves crash against shore, thinks of the many tricks winds off the lake can play on a man, and he sits back, continues to drink and when he hears another noise from the hallway, he thinks maybe it is the booze, but he doesn't stop, can't stop drinking it, and after darkness sets in, he lights two candles, sets them on the table beside him, then lifts the top of the phonograph, chooses a record from the interior storage rack, sees it is Billie Holiday, Edith's favorite, places it on the turntable, and moves the arm to the right, so that the old album will play continuously, and he sits back down, listens to the familiar voice that he has refused to hear since Edith's death, and he remembers the night they had seen Holiday perform in Milwaukee, a concert they had driven over five hours in the fog and rain to see, and he gets up, takes Edith's picture off the wall, looks at her while he continues to drink, Billie Holiday sings, and then the room gets blurry, he is drunk—has he fallen asleep?—he isn't sure, but he starts, sits up straight, suddenly feels a warm breeze sidling beside him like fingertips against his skin and his breathing becomes deeper, he closes his eyes, thinks about the men gone down in that shipwreck, the breeze continues embracing, caressing, he had not meant to start that fire, the old wood burning stove, the spark, the kindling too close, he has lived with the shame, could not save the child that day, or her, or himself, for the rest of their days, those flames rising and swirling, the heat and smoke a horror and he dreams the flames now, wakes screaming, the candles flickering and Holiday still singing the same songs, that sultry voice enticing him back to sleep and then he is with Edith, an old club, dancing, Milwaukee, a slow dance, she is also on stage singing, and he watches her, and he feels now the old tingly feeling he hasn't felt in years, and it is all so vivid, and they are dancing, and there are the three of them now, they hold him, the child's hands in his own, he listens to her sing at the same time, she is singing, he knows, he has left the old record on all night, but it is her, and the people in the bar are his friends, his family, and he looks down and notices that she wears the wedding dress, but he is wearing an old pullover sweater, a short-sleeved work shirt, dirty brown pants, no shoes, and he feels embarrassed, tells her he must go change, but she just laughs, tells him he looks fine, *you look fine, Daddy*, the child, it is her, she is laughing, and they dance, but are outside, it is night and they are alone, beneath stars, he no longer feels cold just an unfamiliar warmth, and she kisses him, says she must leave, and he clings to her, begs her, NO!, but she is fading, fading, and the child hugs him, then they are all but gone, he calls to her frantically, *take me with you, I want to be with you*, and she is gone and he wakes, rubs his eyes, glances around the room—candle wax on the table, he feels warm, a dim light through the windows, morning, and he takes the bottle looks at it and sees that it is less than half full, he doesn't remember drinking that much, he looks for the cork, but can't find it—it isn't on the counter where he'd left it, isn't under his chair, isn't on the stereo cabinet, or under the coffee table, and he finally gives up, covers the bottle with foil, puts it in the refrigerator and then considers going to the bedroom to lie down, but realizes he isn't tired and he looks out the kitchen window, sees the morning covered in fog, can barely make out the shoreline, feels restless, walks outside, heads down the tree-lined road, amazed at his pace, remembers how they used to go to the Dougherty's for barbecues, how he had taught their kids to ride their bikes, given them tours of the lighthouse, told them stories, how they would ride horses on the beach, the many moonlit walks, he and Edith, and long drives together after weekend camping trips, talking about their life together, as if it could never end, and when he arrives at the end of the gravel road, he turns and on the road that led through town, makes his way through the fog, past the park, the Bayside Bar, the neighborhoods and, finally, to the road that leads through the woods, where his walk grows steadier and he is moving effortlessly, until, at last, he is at the cemetery, weaves his way through the remembrances of other people's beloved ones until he is at their graves, the small stone that simply says, Edith Borgeson, 1925-2013, and the one beside it, Abigail, 1949-1952, and he looks down, looks again, disbelief, for there it lay, the cork, and he picks it up, feels the same breeze touch his hand and it is the child, and she points to the trees and he looks where she points and she is there, Edith, motioning for him to follow and when he looks behind him one last time, he can just make out the lighthouse in the fog and he looks down at the child, who leads him toward the woman ahead, into the forest they walk into the forest, the mist, the forest is dressed in mist and as he walks, he wonders who will find the by-then stiffened body and Billie Holiday on the phonograph, singing the same songs, over and over again.

Flight

DUSK WHEN THE plane lifts, and I look down at the country below. Crosshatched land in colors of brown and green, a dull red barn with a silver roof. This flight is carrying me back to where everything began. Home, though that word is a complicated one for me. Above the clouds now, and they move in puffs, wisps of cold and moist touching the tip of the airplane nose, and still we move forward. Strips of white move across the lake, which will be frozen soon, and the snow looks smooth, though I know it isn't. It sustains us, this air, goes unnoticed, even when we fill it with particulate and smog.

The first time I drove to Albuquerque to see her, I was twenty. I remember the skies reaching for forever, and the clouds on the horizon, the desert red sandstone mesas, and the sun going down. Driving through Santa Fe, stuck in traffic, the interstate full of semis, dinner of rellenos, the Indians on the plaza selling bread, red chile ristras hanging from adobe walls. The small house at the end of the road, meeting her mother, drinking hot cocoa and speaking of days in Durango. Her father coming home, happy to meet me, he said. And our drive later through the city that night.

My memory holds us in a convertible, though I never owned such a car. In that memory, she wears a scarf and it flows behind her as we drive, and she has sunglasses, though it is night. Or perhaps that was the sunny afternoon we headed north from Las Cruces, the pecan orchards in neat rows spreading out to the foothills.

And later, in the small apartment with high ceilings where she sat curled on the couch drinking tea, the TV never on, and how I wanted so much to be a part of all I would never understand. How I looked at her, filled with a yearning to fly and be grounded all at the same time.

And the night that lingers most, the ice cold San Luis Valley, Kahlua and coffee, twenty below, and Christine outside in the warmed-up car, waiting as we said goodbye. My cold hands, the sweat, and if I think real hard I can still taste the Kaluah on her lips.

DARK NOW, AND we've passed through the air space of two states. Down there, not far from the lake where we once walked and fed the swans, she is sleeping, her son down the hall, in that cold December city where once we walked through snow falling, holding hands as we made our way down 16th Street, and even then I knew that my love for her would always haunt me. And I wonder if she ever thinks of me now, if she ever fully knew how I felt? And where is that love now? Hunkered down like a soldier in a bunker, hiding from itself and all that hovers to devour it. Like a potato in the cellar, its eyes growing, reaching, bending. As for her, she lives alone, and is lonely, as she was always destined to be, the curse of her own independent will. And this plane will not land there, but will pass overhead, the night so dark that not even our shadow will glaze her rooftop.

In the Long Shadow of a Winter Morning

[1]
Sunday Morning

MORNINGS HE SPLITS wood outside the winter shed, his puffs of breath dissipating slowly into the dark somber air. It comforts him, the rhythmic motion of the ax, the cedar smell, the ripping echo. He stops, removes his fur lined cap, wipes his sweat with the back of his glove.

He imagines her, his daughter, still inside, asleep on the couch. Yesterday, he searched for remnants of himself in her face, but could find nothing. She is her mother's daughter, as seems fair and just. He is an occasional Christmas gift, a monthly support check. Perhaps it's all he'll ever be.

It was a cold dawn in October, that day he left to live alone in the woods with the wind and the chill, an old worn jacket on his back, a bag full of possessions he kept hidden in the trees. It was unforgivable, he knew, leaving his wife and daughter to fend for themselves. There are many ways a man can fail, and he'd found most of them. Those days of drink are still a blur, a drunken accident, his license revoked, and then, the hospital bills, a collection agency, money taken out of Karen's monthly check. They'd run out of propane in their tank, the house had gone cold. He walked away, as a gift, he rationalized then. He was one less mouth for her to feed.

•

MARILYN SITS UP on the couch where she has slept, wraps the blanket around her, takes in the strangeness of the room, the wood burning scent, the fading painting of a mountain man on horseback hanging on the wall. The room is lined with shelves, full of books. This surprises her. She has never imagined her father as a reader, realizes how little she knows about him. She recognizes a ceramic bowl, a gift she once gave him. That was over ten years ago, a project at school. Marilyn has shelves of her own, in her bedroom back home. On one she keeps the Christmas and birthday gifts he has remembered to send—a stuffed polar bear, a soapstone Eskimo dancer, a whale carved from walrus ivory, the complete works of Jack London. ("That's no book for girls," her mother had said with disgust when she opened it. But she read it, every word, most of it twice). The other shelf is empty—the gifts he has failed to send. *Failed*, she needs to believe; not *forgotten*.

Marilyn is seventeen, and lives in Portland with her mother and stepfather. She is back-of-the-room quiet and shy, known and liked by all her classmates. She goes to occasional parties, rarely drinks, tried smoking pot once, hated it. Will try it again, though, she thinks. Why not? She gets good grades, has a boyfriend named Jason, though she has a secret crush on a different boy.

She dresses and walks up the stairs, squinting at the lines of light coming through the window shades. If she were home, she would drive to Cannon Beach, or Cape Meares, take a long walk alone on the beach. She has dreams about the ocean, thinks of becoming a marine biologist. From outside she hears the sound of his hatchet. Or is it an axe. Is there a difference? She isn't sure. She has come to Alaska to see him, to discern a logic for his years of neglect. For years now, she has kept a journal of letters to him, letters which she will never send. She has both loved and hated him, has flipped coins, pulled petals off of flowers. She is here now, here in Alaska, to decide once and for all. Yesterday had not gone well. She is leaning toward hate.

[2]
The Night Before the Last Time She Saw Him

SHE IS TWELVE. From the bathroom window, in the dark, she sees the car parked across the street, knows it's him. She knows that he hopes they will spend the next day together, that he will try to get a leg up on all the horror stories he is sure her mother has told her about him. He will admit some of them are true, people make mistakes, he is different now. He will imagine the two of them, father and daughter, laughing over dinner, seeing the animals at the zoo, shopping at downtown gift shops. She can't bear it, the thought of the whole day. She calls her two best friends, Mary and Lindy, invites them along.

[3]
Back in January

JANET, HIS EX, calls him from Portland. It's not even the fifteenth yet, he thinks, what the hell.

"The check's in the mail," he says, as soon as he recognizes her voice. This is true. He has not been late on a payment in over five years. But that's not why she's called.

"She wants to come see you, against my better judgment," she says.

He has to think for a minute, unsure who she's talking about, something for which he immediately feels shame.

"Why?" he asks.

"Gee, Robert, I don't know. Maybe she thinks a girl should know her father. If it's a problem—"

"When?" he asks. He tries to imagine her now grown up, realizes he knows her only as a child.

"Spring break," says Janet. "Last week of March."

[4]
Yesterday

SHE ARRIVES ON the mail plane. She sits in the co-pilot's seat, looking at the ground below as it slowly comes closer and closer. Finally, the small tires hit the snow-covered gravel runway, she feels the force of the landing pulling her tightly against the back of her seat, until the plane comes to a rolling halt. With the pilot's help, she steps out of the plane. She sees him then, a large man with a red beard. Her father. He wears a fur-lined hat, and an old gray jacket. His smallness doesn't match her memory. He has a rough, weather-worn face, wrinkles around his eyes. He hugs, awkwardly, unsure. He helps the pilot unload her bags from the plane. She walks to the edge of the runway, peers out at the lake, the mountains beyond. She feels the cold wind on her face, the stinging bite. The world is covered with snow here, even this late in March. Alaska, she thinks.

She waves thanks to the pilot, watches the plane turn, accelerate. Her father moves to stand beside her, and together they watch as the plane takes off and disappears into the late afternoon sky.

He has made way too much food, a feast of caribou steaks and sourdough bread, Jell-O salad and potatoes with gravy. She only eats a small portion of the heaping plateful he gives her.

She asks the usual questions—polar bears and Eskimos and igloos, and he has to explain that's all further north, that people don't actually live in igloos. He hopes to show her the northern lights, but when they walk outside later, all they see are the stars. They stand looking up at the Alaskan winter sky.

"There are so many!" she says, impressed, and he thinks maybe the stars are enough.

[5]
The Night Before the Last Time He Saw Her

IT'S 1996. SHE is in sixth grade, skinny and shy, vulnerable, he thinks, without him in her life. It is October, his one break between his dual jobs of guiding summer fishing trips and winter care-taking at the lodge. He is sober now, has not had a drink in over a year. He has flown down only to see her, though he tells Janet he is in Portland on business. He has rented a car, reserved a room in the nearest motel he can find. The night before his scheduled visit, he drives to the house, parks across the street. It is raining, coming down in steady waves over his old neighborhood, with the single story box frame houses. The yards are small, and neatly trimmed, with large trees—maple, cascades, paperbark. Through his rain-soaked window, he stares at the house he himself once owned. There is light from the living room that faces the street. Occasionally, he sees silhouetted movement passing behind the curtains. An upstairs bedroom light comes on. He thinks of her up there, his daughter. Soon she will be a teenager. Her childhood is ending, and he has missed it.

He sits in the rain and waits, watching, until all of the lights in the house go dark.

[6]
Yesterday

THEY ARE STANDING, looking up at the Alaskan winter sky.

"You know," she says by way of introducing the subject they have both been avoiding. "Mom has never forgiven you."

"She hasn't, huh?" he says. "What about you?"

"The jury's still out." She pauses, lets him think about that. "She says that God owes her three years at the end of her life for the years she spent living with you."

"Really." He isn't sure what to say to that. "I don't think it works that way. There's two sides to everything." He looks at the winter shed, realizes one of the outside lights has burnt out. Forgiveness, he thinks. A very underrated human characteristic. If she could have forgiven him, he could have made it right.

"So now's your chance," Marilyn says. "What's your side?"

He looks at her. "My side? My side is that people fall in and out of love. We fell in, then we fell out." He stops, realizes how trite that sounds. *Had* he fallen out of love with her? He thinks back to the last time he saw Karen, how standing in that small living room, looking at her, how beautiful she still seemed to him, that sinking feeling of loss, of all that he had thrown away. "Mistakes," he says. "People make mistakes, you know." He sighs. "I made a lot of mistakes."

"So, basically, you fucked up, then?" she says.

He looks at her, narrows his eyes, looks back to the sky.

"Does Barry let you talk like that?"

"Barry doesn't really tell me what to do," she says.

"If I'd been around," he says, "you'd know better than to talk like that."

"Well that's really the whole point, isn't it. Dad."

An old anger rises inside him, but he holds it all in. He wants to reply, to explain, to tell her...what? He doesn't know. She waits through his silence, and when he doesn't break it, she turns and walks into the lodge, the screen door slamming behind her.

He stands on the porch, watching the sky, watching his breath disappear into the night, listening to the wind brush through the trees. He craves a cigarette, wishes to hell he still smoked.

[7]
On the Day He Last Saw Her

He wakes in his hotel room, showers, splashes aftershave on his face. He is happy, nervous. Resolves to be patient and charming, forgiving of the past. Contrite. This is a new beginning, he thinks. He can't know that it will be five years before he will see her again. He drives to the house, gets there early, drives around the block a few times. Gray clouds move swiftly across the sky, water drips from the neighborhood trees, from the eaves of the houses. A woman he vaguely recognizes walks a pair of white poodles.

Finally, he parks in front of the house, walks to the door. A man answers, Janet's second husband. The man wears a blue denim shirt with his name stitched on the pocket. Barry. He holds a cigarette between his fingers, moves it to his mouth to shake Robert's hand.

"Come in," he says. "I think they're about ready."

They? he wonders. Surely Janet won't be joining them.

But it's not Janet. Robert is disappointed to find that Marilyn has invited two of her sixth-grade friends.

"Dad, that's lame," says Marilyn when he suggests the zoo. The other girls laugh. They spend the day at a video arcade, the girls giggling and playing games, drinking sodas, huddling together, whispering.

In the late afternoon, they go to a mall. He stays back, tries not to hover, spends a lot of time standing awkwardly, pretending to look at merchandise in the stores they pass.

He tries to think of witty things to say, tries to imagine how to impress sixth-grade girls. He has spent the last two years living alone in the Alaskan bush. The mall crowd is making him dizzy. He feels disoriented, out of touch. All that's inside of him tremors. At the food court, the deep- fried, sticky, syrupy scent makes him nauseous. His head throbs, and he feels a sharp pain in his stomach.

For dinner, they go out for pizza. The girls are talking, all three at once. They whisper, point at boys, giggle amongst themselves. Rarely do they talk to him.

"He's so weird," he overhears Marilyn say, probably talking about a boy in their class, he consoles himself. But he feels his heart sink.

It's not until the evening, after he's dropped the girls off, that he is alone in the car with her.

"It's nice to be back in Portland," he says. She doesn't reply. For a long time they drive in silence. Ice cream, he thinks. Coffee. Cream pie at the Village Inn. Anything. But it is almost eight o'clock now, time for her to be home. "No later," Janet had said, glaring at him. Court order, he thinks.

"Did you have a good time?" he asks as he drops her off.

"Yes," she says, but in a tone that is less than convincing. He watches as she walks up the sidewalk and into the house, never once looking back at him. He sits, wondering if he should go inside, talk to Janet. He wonders if the back bedroom outlet ever got fixed, if the bathtub still drips. He wonders if Janet finally got the bedroom furniture she had always wanted. He thinks how, if he still lived here, he would put a hedge beneath the living room window, plant a couple of trees.

Finally, he puts the rental in drive, and makes his way back to the motel, passes the bars along the way without stopping. He lies in bed, the cable TV sound down, flickering images casting a glow throughout the room. Unable to sleep, he leaves the motel, walks through the darkness of night, through the streets of the city. There are other people walking, passing him. He hears the dim sound of a jukebox, moves toward it, until he sees the neon in the window. He leans against a brick wall directly across the street from the bar. He is breathing heavily, feels the thumping of his heart. Walk away, he thinks, walkawaywalkawaywalkaway and he does. A few blocks further, he realizes he is shaking, takes deep breaths to steady himself. He turns, walks back. Thinks of his daughter, her friends, their laughter, he has no reason not to go forward, he can already feel the next morning's remorse, it is inevitable, out of his control, and he stops, has to catch his breath. A man approaches. The man is wearing an old worn jacket. Robert can smell the sour scent of the man's breath, the reek of his own past in the man's clothes.

"Spare some cash?" says the man, and Robert pulls a wad from his pocket, gives it all to the man.

"Buy some food," he says to the man, and he puts his hand on the man's shoulder, and pulls him toward him until their foreheads gently touch. They pull away, and their eyes meet, and the man nods. The gratitude is mutual. Robert turns, heads directly to the motel.

[8]
Yesterday

MARILYN WALKS INTO the lodge, the door slamming behind her, lies down on the couch in the living room. Did he deserve that? she wonders. At one time he did. Deserved worse. It will always be there, she thinks, this gap of years we've missed. No way to deny it. It will be there in all that she ever does, in each boy she dates, in every relationship she has, the gap will never be filled. It is as if someone had tried to plant roses, but had accidentally planted poison ivy instead, and then the plants spread, grew so thick, the roots spread so deep, that no one could weed through them, no one could clear the space to retry the roses. The best you could do was keep cutting the ivy back, knowing that it would continue to grow, to spread. It was hopeless, maybe. The only way to change the present is to change the past, but it's always too late. She hates him, she decides, once and for all. They say that love is redemptive, but it is hate that will allow her to let go, hate that was her only hope to move on. If she hates him, she won't have to care anymore. Goodbye, Daddy. She will write it in her journal, the only two words of a final letter to him. And then she will burn them all on a fire on the beach, first chance she gets once she gets home.

HE STANDS, CALMING himself. Deep breaths, he thinks. A gust of wind moves through the treetops, and he feels the chill of the blown snow on his neck. He turns, moves toward the house, throws open the screen, the door banging against the side of the house. He walks down the stairway, and into the one room basement, where she sits pretending to read on the corner of the old couch.

"You can't come here and talk to me like that, you understand me. You think it's okay to hate me, but you have no right to hate me."

She holds her ground. "Okay, Robert," she says calmly. "I won't hate you. How could I? I don't really know you. Case closed. Can I read now, please?"

"Don't do that! Your mother used to do that. Don't treat me like I don't matter. I'd rather you hate me."

"Fine. I hate you. Happy?"

Deep breaths, he thinks. "You need to treat me with more respect while you're here. I deserve that much."

"Deserve? Are you kidding me? I don't owe you anything. Why would I ever show respect for you?"

"I'm your father."

"By blood, only. You should know, I consider Barry my father—"

"Yes, by blood! And that should mean enough. You don't know.…There are things you don't know…"

"Is this where you're going to start turning me against Mom. Because you can forget it. I hate this place! How do you live here? There's nothing to do. I want to go home."

He stands, glaring, breathing hard. He looks for himself in her face, in her eyes, the cleft of her chin. Nothing. She is all her mother. All over again. He looks down, squeezes his eyes tight.

"You do what you have to do," he says. "The number's by the phone. If you want to leave, just call Sandy at Peninsula Air. Tell her to have Dave come get you when he flies back in the afternoon. If that's what you want."

"That's what you want, isn't it," she says. "To just get rid of me, it's what you have always wanted."

"The number's by the phone," he says. And he walks up the stairs, and out the front door.

He walks through the snow, to the edge of the lake. He reaches down, digs through the snow until he finds a rock, and he hurls it, throws it as hard as he can, wants to hear the shattering of ice when it lands. Instead, he hears only a single sullen thud, a soft landing in the snow on the ice-covered lake.

"I'd hate me, too," he mutters.

It is nearly an hour before she hears the screen door open, the footsteps on the stairs, hears him, this man, her father, walk into the room. She lies down, closes her eyes, pretends to be asleep. He walks to her, she can feel him standing, watching. Then he walks away, and she hears a closet door open, then close. He moves back to the couch, places a blanket over her, then another. He tucks the blanket gently around her shoulders, sits at the edge of the couch. She feels him breathing next to her.

Then she feels his breath near her face, his lips lightly kissing her forehead.

"I'm sorry," he whispers. She doesn't stir. Try saying that when you don't think I'm asleep, she thinks. Two different silences separate them. He rises, turns off the lights, walks up the stairs. She lies in the dark listening to the stillness of the Alaskan night, the slow dripping of the kitchen water faucet, the clock, ticking one steady second at a time.

[9]
Nights Spent Between January and Her Arrival

FOR WEEKS AFTER Janet calls him, he examines the old pictures, school photos she long ago stopped sending. He sips coffee and tries to imagine Marilyn now, as a seventeen-year-old. On his satellite TV he watches music videos and fears the worst—tattoos, multiple piercings, hair dyed purple and green. He wants to save her, he realizes, but from what? The boys at her school? All of the unseen dangers that lurk for a young woman in the world? He looks out the window and realizes the truth, what it is he wants. Too late, he thinks, and from outside the wind rattles the pane, and he thinks of ice at the bottom of an empty glass, of chattering teeth, of a mouthful of blood after a fall.

SHE IS LYING on her bed, her headphones on, the volume turned high. She will lose her hearing someday, her mother keeps saying it, and who cares, who cares. It will be a welcome break from the endless noise, the teachers, and parents and TVs and the boys, the boys like Jason, who has now, just now, on the phone, called her a "psychobitch," and she has slammed down the receiver, and then taken it off the hook, and she will never understand them, the boys, not now, not when they become men. She knows who to blame, and she writes it all down, all that she wants to tell him when she gets there, to Alaska. She has a memory glimpse of a night long ago, she was a child, lying in bed. She could hear pounding on the locked door, and her mother's voice, go away, go away, go away. Then, red and blue lights moving in circles across the ceiling above her, her father's strange voice—*Let me see my daughter, my daughter*—all fading into silence in the night.

[10]
Today. The Present

SHE IS UP now, he hears her inside, hears the screen door open. He stops, takes a sip from his coffee.

"Mornin'," he says.

She says nothing, but sits on a stump across from where he chops. The sun is rising now, the orange glow reflecting on the frozen lake in the distance.

He doesn't speak again, doesn't look up. Continues the chopping of the wood.

"You chopped all this?" she asks, finally, looking at the wood, piled high against all four shed walls, two and three rows deep.

"It's a lot of work, taking care of a lodge up here," he says. He splits another log, and then he stops, stretches his back.

He looks at her. Her light brown hair is rumpled around her face. Her red ski jacket is unzipped, and beneath she wears a gray sweatshirt. He sees her mother, he thinks, in the eyes, her chin, the rounded curve of her cheek bones. She has his brown hair, though, and narrow lips.

"Drink coffee?" he asks.

"Maybe just juice," she says.

"There's orange juice in the refrigerator," he tells her. She nods, but doesn't move. She watches him from her seat on the stump, the sunlight now casting long morning shadows in the snow.

"You want to carry some of this and stack it?" he asks.

She shrugs, and he helps her load an armful, carry it to the pile.

"You're strong," he says.

"Yeah, right. Do I get that from you?"

He shakes his head. "Naw, your mother. I used to be amazed at what she could do." The sun is rising higher, now. The sparkling snow hurts her eyes, and he watches her rub them, thinks about those tiny baby hands, years ago, gripping his finger as he held her.

"Did you ever love Mom?" she asks.

"Of course—I always loved her." He feels himself blush as he says the word, and laughs—such a rugged Alaskan man.

"Still?" she asks.

"I don't know." He takes a swing with the axe, and she watches as the two evenly split pieces fall to the ground. "I still love who she was when I knew her, still love the memory of her." He chuckles. "Besides, she has Barry now."

"Barry. God. He's such a dweeb," she says.

Robert smiles to himself. "He treats you good, though, right?"

"I don't know. I guess. There are no roads here. What do you do, walk everywhere?" she asks.

"No. Snow machines."

"Snow machines?"

"You know, snowmobiles. You ever ride one?"

"Dad, I live in Portland." She rises, takes an axe, from the wall. Sets a log on the stump, and awkwardly attempts to split it.

He stops, watches her. "Here, use this one," he says and they trade axes.

"There's a lot of places to ride around Portland, actually," he says.

She shrugs. "They're noisy, right? And, besides, they're bad for the environment."

He looks at her, deadpan. "Yeah. It would be better if we built roads so we could have cars out here. Then we wouldn't be ruining nature with our snow machines."

"That's real nice," she says.

"So you don't want to ride one, then. That's fine."

She thinks. "I guess I wouldn't mind riding one. Where do you go?"

"Anywhere you want. I use them to gather wood, to hunt, to check traps."

Marilyn doesn't respond, and he wonders if maybe he shouldn't have brought up the trapping, the killing of animals. No telling what they fill these kids' minds with in the big city.

"You hunt?" she asks, finally.

"You'll notice there's not exactly a Safeway across the lake. You ever shot a gun?"

"Uh, no."

"Now, there's something I can teach you. Trust me the boys'll love you."

"Yeah, whatever." She watches him, the steady rhythm with which he works. She hears the thrusts of breath released from his lungs as his ax hits the wood. She tries to match him. "Did Mom ever shoot guns?"

"No. That's why I'm still here on this earth." They stop, and he wipes his brow, takes off his jacket and hangs it on a nail on the wall. "Hey," he says. "She never taught you to dance, did she?"

"No."

"Phew. You're lucky. That's one thing she couldn't do. Graceful, gorgeous, the most amazing person I've ever known. But she couldn't put that all to music. Do you two-step?"

"Not really."

"I'll teach you. Tonight, I'll teach you. How's that?"

"I don't know about all this," she says, and she imagines it, speeding through the snow, shooting guns, two-stepping with her father inside an Alaskan lodge beneath the northern lights.

"You still have a lot to learn, too, you know," she says.

"I know," he says.

"I'm not going to let you off so easy," she says.

"It's a conclusion I've already arrived at," he says.

Soon, she is chopping with a steady rhythm. He watches, nods at her. They spend the morning this way, father and daughter, together splitting wood, the percussive beat of their chore echoing through the wilderness, their mutual exhalations merging and rising, disappearing into the crisp Alaskan air.

Where We Land

My name is Mitchell Jensen, and before I bought this boat and moved up here to Alaska for good, I spent three seasons playing quarterback for three different teams in the National Football League. Before you start sifting through your trading cards, let me spare you the trouble; I won't be there. Not a lot of third-stringers get cards made of them. Or posters, or bobble-head dolls, or Slurpee cups, or fan jerseys with their name on the back. Unless you're a die-hard Copley State fan (and if you are, I know you by name), you haven't heard of me. My pro highlight reel consists of about forty-five minutes of pre-season games, with voice-overs of bored broadcasters talking about how this is the time for the good players to not get hurt. It's those forty-five minutes that kept me in the league all that time—not bad really, for a poor stiff who started his senior season second-string at a Division II school.

It's the end of August, and already the mountainsides across Kachemak are dotted with yellow and red. The water is lazy smooth, and the white of distant glacier shimmers at the edge of the bay. Most of the tourist boats are gone, and even though I can see the lodge in the cliffs, it feels like we have Tutka Bay to ourselves. The pinks were biting all morning, even though it's late in the season. Earlier, out past Point Pogibshi, four fin whales passed less than fifty feet from where we sat anchored. We've just finished a lunch of caribou sausage with cheddar on crackers, and pineapple bits, washed down with orange cream sodas. Buddha belches. He's sitting on a deck chair, knitting.

Buddha is Buddha Faleomavaega, from Samoa. He knits, he says, because he needs to keep his hands busy. Best offensive lineman Copley State ever had, probably, but definitely the best fishing buddy. You want to catch fish—trust me on this—hang out with a Samoan.

"Ready to head back?" I ask him.

"Naw, man. Stay me here," he says. "Throw me in. I'll live with the mermaids."

"You making me a hat?" I ask.

"A Christmas sweater," he says. "Wait til she sees it." And I know right away, he's talking about Tina. A hopeless situation. The mermaid dream might be better odds.

I raise the anchor, start the engine.

IN MY THREE years, I played in exactly one regular season play, a gimmick that garnered my team a five-yard loss. Not my fault, trust me. That play wouldn't have worked in a Pee Wee League game. I think part of the reason I was in on that play to begin with was because the other two quarterbacks refused to have anything to do with it. The few times that my name was in the news, it was usually when the 1st stringer got hurt, and the report said something like, "If QB Number Two gets hurt, the team will have to rely on (gasp!) Mitchell Jensen." Once, the first two quarterbacks did get hurt. There were two minutes to go in the game, we were down by twenty, and I figured what the hell, I'll get to air one out, maybe. I put on my helmet, was ready to go. So what did our brilliant coach do? He put a reserve halfback in to run out the clock with quick snaps.

But I'm not bitter. The NFL is the NFL. Even if you're the worst quarterback on the worst team in the league, you're still one of the best in the world.

Anyway, this is not really about football. It's some about Alaska and fishing. And my father, I guess. And, because I'm a twenty-eight-year-old retired quarterback who spends summers on a boat with a man named Buddha, you've probably already figured this out:

This is about a woman.

Renita Lewis runs llama treks out of the Matunuska Valley. I like to think she's up on a mountainside right now looking out over a field of wildflowers trying to make up her mind once and for all about me. But the truth is, she's probably not thinking about me at all. She's probably too busy making sure tired tourists and persnickety pack animals all get along. Renita's amazing that way. She's an animal lover first, people handler second. She claims to not really like people at all, and men even less, but I've seen her charm her way to tips you wouldn't believe. When I first told her I'd played in the NFL, she shrugged and said, "I dated a Congressman from Utah once." The good thing about that conversation is that it left me so flummoxed, I never even had to explain the whole third-string thing.

I COULD COACH, I really could. Every mistake my coaches ever made, I knew before they did. *That play won't work,* I often thought but never said. I was rarely wrong. I have no desire to coach, though. My father was a coach, so I know the headaches.

"You can't just be glad to be there," my father used to say. But I was. I was always just glad to be there. For showing up, practicing, watching film, holding a clipboard, and running one dud play in a meaningless game, I made just over a million dollars, invested most of it, am doing okay. I have a small condo in Anchorage, a cabin in Colorado. I live on this boat whenever I can, which is pretty much all summer. I'll have to find work eventually, I know. But for now, I'm content. I charter a little bit, for tourists, when I feel like it, and sometimes take extra bookings from some of the other charters when they get busy. It's been almost two years since I've been back to Florida, where my parents live. But I can't go back. I check flights, see the prices, rehearse in my head the conversation that waits for me there.

"I get Alaska, I really do," said my mother the last time I talked to her. "But the winter? Sweety, we're not cold weather people. You should come home."

And then, "He forgives you, you know." Nice to hear, but I think she has the equation backward. And I want to say so, that I'm not the one that needs to be forgiven.

"I'll think about it," I say. But I've already decided, I'll freeze first, before I go back there.

I met Renita at Humpy's on a Monday night. I noticed her right away, as soon as she walked in. To my surprise, she came and sat at the bar stool beside me, which seemed a good sign at the time. But my initial flirtations were met with bewilderment, then disdain. I pulled out all the stops, and she blocked me at every turn.

I started with the beauty of her eyes, which, okay, was a line, but also happens to be true.

"That's just the contacts I wear," she said dismissively.

When she told me she had a golden retriever, I told her I planned on getting one myself, which is the truth.

"If that were true you'd already have one," she said. "But I'll tell you what, I know someone at the retriever rescue. His name is Nate. Call him. I'm sure he'll be happy to help you out."

"You should let me make you dinner. I'm a really good chef," I said.

"Jesus," she said. "Really?"

"C'mon," I said. "Play nice for five minutes."

She sighed. "Okay," she said, "What do you do?"

"I'm kind of between things," I said.

"Of course you are," she said. That's when I told her about the NFL, and she pulled out the whole congressman from Utah thing. I was never good at this, the bar talk. When she wouldn't let me buy her I drink, I disgusted myself by playing the pity card.

"Look," I said, "I'm just trying to talk. I'm a long way from home, I'm lonely, and it wouldn't hurt you to be nice. And by the way," I said, "I was sitting here first. If you didn't want my company, why did you sit next to me?"

She looked at me for a long time, and then she laughed.

"Well, goddamn, Cowboy. A refreshingly heartfelt moment."

Okay, the laugh was sarcastic, but it lit up the room. I considered it progress.

"I sat next to you, because the seat was empty. Do you always assume every woman who sits by you wants a piece?"

The heartfelt honest answer to that question was "no." No, I don't assume that at all. Has. Not. Been. My. Experience.

We did talk, long enough for me to learn she too had once lived in Florida, had moved to Alaska after the house she owned burned down, a tragedy she shrugged off as a minor inconvenience. She had worked on a fishing boat for a while, and then for an outfitter that flew bear trips out of Kodiak. Anchorage, she said, was a good place to drink and to shop, but she lived near Palmer, in a dry cabin. She played violin in a bluegrass band. I was smitten.

I had to beg, but I talked her into coffee at Kaladi's the next day. I wasn't convinced she would show, but she did. When she told me about her llamas, I booked the trip, a two-nighter with six strangers. She spent the whole time charming them and ignoring me. Watching her on that trip, I fell deeply into the can't-sleep-at-night-every-song-was-written-about-us swoon. When we returned on the final day to the trailhead and parking lot, she agreed to join me for dinner the next night, on the terms that I not call it a date. This is how it works with me. When I say that I played in the NFL, what I mean is that I didn't play at all. When I say that I am dating the love of my life, what I mean is that I'm not. It's just all a lot of standing on sidelines. No, Dad, I think, I'm not just happy to be here. But it's where I am.

THE WORST QUARTERBACK on the worst team in the league. That's what Buddha still calls me. If he knew it bothered me, he'd never say it, so I don't let on.

"Rich," I say, "from a man who knits as a hobby." At this he smiles. It's an old joke, no longer funny if it ever was. In college, he'd knit on road trips, took all kinds of ribbing with an unnerving calm. Unflappable.

We don't joke—or talk at all, really, not anymore—about the knee injury that ended his career. It led to his fifth knee surgery in three years. The difference between millions and nothing sometimes comes down to one meaningless play in the second-to-last game of your college career. He was good—better at his position than I ever was at mine. If he's bitter, he never shows it. I bought this boat with money I earned not playing football games. But, before that, for three years at Copley, Buddha protected my blind side faithfully. The title of this boat's in my name, but I figure Buddha owns a large part of it.

A COUPLE WEEKS ago, Renita and I went on a long morning hike into the Chugachs, and after we were sitting in the café at New Sagaya's. I made the mistake of asking her over to my condo, told her I'd make us dinner.

"I can never sleep with you," she told me. "I think I should be up front about that." It had been months since we'd started doing this thing she doesn't allow me to call dating.

"Why?" I asked.

"I can see what it would do to you. It's too bad," she said looking me up and down. I took that last part as a compliment. The first part, not so much. Perfect, I thought. The only quarterback in NFL history who can't get laid because the sex would not be meaningless enough to him.

"A shame," says Buddha, now, as we make our slow way back to Homer. "I hear she's a bouncing terror in the sack." Says this with a straight face. I always know when Buddha's joking, because it's the only time he doesn't smile. It's the word "bouncing" I think, that gets me. I try not to show it, but I don't always think Buddha's funny.

Buddha, you should know, has his own love problems. He's in love with a woman named Tina who's in love with the high school football coach in Soldotna. Tina's from Hawaii.

"She's a Pacific Islander, like me," he says. "We're perfect for each other. The football coach is just exotic to her right now. She'll come around." Buddha has slept with Tina. More than once. Meaningful. Trust me on this—despite what you might believe about us, men are hopeless saps when it comes to love.

It's important you know this about Renita: she doesn't believe in marriage. "It's obsolete," she says. "Trust me, if I ever want kids, I'll get them." *Get*, she says. Not *have*. I imagine her snatching babies from cribs.

If my football prowess was mediocre, my attempts at love have been absolutely abysmal. The summer after my third season, I was engaged to a woman, Carrie, who saved us both from our inevitable divorce by leaving me at the altar. Later I found out she'd been sleeping with a rival tight end. I'll spare his name, but you've heard of him. This also happened to be the year I was cut for good during training camp. I moved back to Florida, to the town where my parents still live. That fall, my father sat daily by the phone, waiting for a call I knew wasn't coming. I'd done the math. There are new hotshot quarterbacks coming into the league every year. And good old ones hanging on. And about a million in between. I knew where I stood on the national depth chart, but Dad encouraged me to go to the gym, encouraged me to study film, encouraged me to have my agent make calls. Until one day, my agent called and told me I needed to talk to my father. Apparently, Dad had been calling my agent berating him for not getting me a job. Threatened to fire him, which, A) my father couldn't do on authority; and, B) my father couldn't do because I was no longer my agent's client, on account I no longer had a job. Every Tuesday that year, my father called to go over the injury report with me. "Klining's out two games at least," he'd say. "You better call, let them know you're available." My refusal infuriated him.

When I say my father "encouraged" me, what I mean is he verbally held every failure he'd ever known against me. There was yelling. Accusations. By mid-October, the whole thing devolved into a shouting match. He laid out every mistake I'd ever made—the fumbles, the mis-reads, the nights spent at movies rather than at the gym. And it wasn't just football, but also the report cards, the "frivolous" art classes—I once liked to paint and draw—and then he started in about Carrie. I see now that with Carrie and me, it probably just wasn't meant to be, but the public humiliation of it, the having to return all of those gifts, well. You might say it stung me. It doesn't excuse what I did, I know.

Anyway, Dad was standing in the kitchen entryway, and I was sitting at the table, and his face was red. I saw the veins in his neck, and he was standing over me, and he had to bring Carrie into it, and I just lost it. I stood and I shoved him, knocked him hard against the wall. He started to throw a punch, so I slugged him.

"Mitchell! Stop it," said my mom. I didn't know she'd walked in the room. I like to think I never would have done it had I known she was there, but before that moment I would never have believed myself capable of such a thing at all. He looked at me, breathing heavy, and he wiped his nose with the back of his hand, looked down at the blood then at me, a look that said everything I ever was or would be was coated in failure.

That's when I bought the cabin in Colorado, sight unseen, and moved out of my parents' town, away from Florida for good. After the long drive, I spent two months in that cabin, drinking gin under the stars at night. Alone. I rarely went to the nearby town, which was just a gas station and grocery store, one small café. I let the battery in my cell phone go dead, and didn't bother to re-charge it. I had all my mail forwarded to a post office box in Colorado Springs, which I rarely checked.

By then, Buddha had already moved to Alaska. When we talked, usually during a drunken phone call I made at a pay phone at an abandoned but nearby lodge, all he ever talked about was how perfect it was. I made the move the following spring, not even sure I was really doing it, just driving. But I'd packed my car full, and drove for nearly ten days. I sat in the hot springs in a place called Liard. Somewhere in the Yukon I watched a grizzly cub playing in the middle of the highway. One night in a hotel bar in Whitehorse, I was watching ESPN and learned that my ex's tight end had been traded to a division where the defenses were notoriously physical. I secretly hoped for an injury, which in fact happened four games into the next season when he broke his leg. On a whim, I drunk dialed my ex from my hotel room, and heard a crazy man I didn't recognize scream profanities into the phone at her. The next morning I drove fifteen straight hours all the way to Anchorage, where I fell asleep in my car while parked at a Carr's grocery store, and was woken by a man who offered me drugs. He was standing outside my door, and I angrily opened the door so hard that I knocked him to the pavement. I threatened him, fully expecting him to pull a gun on me. Instead he got up and ran. Exhausted I rested for two days in an Anchorage hotel, never leaving my room, until I finally called Buddha.

"You have to come to Homer," he said. "Homer will heal you." So I headed out to the Kenai. It was the drive around Turnagain Arm that started it, I think. It was sunny, those mountains rising over Cook Inlet. Dall sheep on the roadside. I drove, stopping once to hike through brush so thick I had to part it with my arms as I moved over the trail. Later, past Ninilchick, I pulled over and looked across the water at two triangular shaped peaks, which, I learned later, are still-active volcanoes. I felt calm for the first time in as long as I could remember. By the time I saw the sign in Homer that said "The End of the Road," I'd already decided I was staying. A week later, I was walking on the docks when I saw the For Sale sign attached to this boat, a 1996 Bayliner Avanti. It was like everything I've ever done suddenly made sense. Shortly after that, I met Renita.

Besides knitting, Buddha is a master potter. Last year I helped him build an anagama kiln behind his small house. It's a wood-burning kiln, with small chambers where you stack the pieces on shelves. The ashes from the wood create a natural glaze. He makes vases, mugs, large bowls. They're really stunningly beautiful. Iridescent is the word he uses. Last year he had a show at a gallery in Homer, and he sold several vases, one for three hundred dollars. I don't think I've ever seen him happier.

I asked him once how he dealt with the injury, the knowledge that his pro football dreams were over. He just shrugged.

"It was a crapshoot, anyway," he said. "Who knows? A lot of those guys are so screwed up. Maybe if I'd played, I'd have done coke. Or steroids. Or hookers. Too much money, too much time, too much that feeds an ego. Or, maybe I would've started a charity and saved poor sick children." He shrugged. "There's no such thing as luck, good or bad," he says. "There's just life. I fish and knit and throw pots. It's fine."

THE WEEK AFTER the llama trek, I invited Renita over to the condo one night when I was in Anchorage. Nothing major, I said. Salmon on the grill, a little wine. Told her Buddha would be there, which is a draw—everyone likes Buddha. I watched her as she sat out on the small deck, laughing, listening to him talk about Samoa, about throwing pots. I was a little jealous at first, but I noticed that she was talking to me more, seemed to be happy. The sarcasm had softened. At one point, she was leaning back against the railing, and the light was behind her, Cook Inlet in the distance. She was laughing, sipping wine, and I watched her run her hand through her hair, behind her ear. It's the image of her I carry with me most when I'm out on the water. Later, after Buddha left, we talked about Alaska, about llamas, about fishing, about Florida.

"I think you are starting to love me, just a little bit," I said, joking, but hopeful, too.

"Love, ha," she said. "It's like God. I'll believe in it when I experience it. In the meantime, it's all social construct."

"Love is definitely real," I said. "I mean, how do you not believe in love?"

"It's not that I do or don't believe, it's just that until I experience it, I can't really know, you know?"

"You've never been in love? I mean, ever, not even a crush on a boy?" I was incredulous. "And, you don't think there's a God?"

"I don't know, I mean it's interesting to me, the concept, but I've just never felt anything like how I hear people describe it. Besides, who needs it? And, God. Here's what I think about her. If there is a God, she's a frustrated artist, and like all frustrated artists, she can never quite get it right, can never quite get the vision she sees in her mind to actually appear on the earth. I mean, humans? What a mess we are. Every artist I know at various points wants to just take all they've been working on, and smash it against the wall. That's what I think hurricanes are."

"That's one crazy theology," I said. But I knew what she meant. I once saw Buddha take a pot out of his kiln, and throw it in disgust against the brick wall at the back of his yard, the pieces shattering against it. My whole life, I had seen the temper tantrums of coaches, my father among them, trying to create on the field what they saw in their visions.

Renita was standing in my kitchen, then, wine glass in her hand. She seemed sad, and I thought I had touched a nerve somehow, that maybe there was a past she couldn't cop to, or think about, or deal with. But I knew better than to ask. I wanted to kiss her, just to force her to push me away, but before I could muster the courage, she suggested we go for a walk. We walked all the way to Point Woronzof, nearly seven

miles out and back, and by the time we returned, we were exhausted. She said goodnight, and I watched her drive away.

"I STAYED WITH Tina last night," says Buddha. He sighs. "I
need to not do that anymore. Not until she loves me. Without
love, it's just perverse, man."

I can see the Homer Spit coming into view, see the figures
walking the shore, a golden lab, returning regally the stick
they've been throwing. The boat hits a wave, water spraying
us. I hear the call of a kittiwake.

"What if she never does?" I ask. I immediately regret it,
but I push on. "What if she never loves you?"

I see the Tustumena ferry in the distance. For a long time,
Buddha says nothing.

"This life is so full of beauty and heartbreak, man," he
says, finally, and I want him to say more, but we ride the water
to dock in silence.

IN THE NIGHT I have a dream that I've had versions of before.
The pro team I'm playing on is down 27 in the fourth quarter.
It is the conference championship game, and the first- and
second-string quarterbacks both get injured. I am inserted
into the game, and I bring us back. First I throw a strike inside the five that sets up a touchdown run. Then, we get the
ball back, and I run, breaking tackles, getting loose along the
sideline, and scoring. The crowd is suddenly invigorated. Next,
we get a fumble, and immediately, I throw a strike to a receiver on a cross pattern. When next we get the ball back, there
are two minutes. I brilliantly work the clock, and on the last
play throw high to a leaping receiver who makes the catch at

the back of the end zone. We win, and the crowd is on the field and the reporters surround me, and there is chaos and confetti, and my heart is pounding. Then there is a TV camera shot, a close up of my parents, and my father is hugging my mother, and the camera moves to a close-up of his face, and he is crying, my father is crying, and I see that he is proud.

I wake, and outside it is raining. The boat bobs gently. The ocean is breathing, I think, the shifting waves like heartbeats. And I am surrounded by water, water below, water falling from the sky. I drift in the breath of it all, in the center of the heartbeat of the sad watery world.

It's no small thing making it to the NFL, and I am in the Copley State Hall of Fame. You could say I've been lucky. Or you could say my career was a failure. I am in love, a feeling that carries its own good fortune. Deep down I know she will probably never love me back. I like how I live, like to say the words: *I live on a boat*. But my father hears this and feels disappointment at who I've become. In three years I made money that guys I played with made in a week. But I drink with people who will never make as much in a lifetime. On this boat, I am free. Free from screaming crowds, free from Florida. Free from fortune.

"Fortune," says Buddha, "begins and ends with conception, and then you are born. That's all the luck you ever need."

Last August, a year ago, Renita invited me on a backpacking excursion to Denali National Park. We rode the bus about fifty miles, and then hiked in along a riverbed until we were beyond the view of the road. Then we made our way up a slope. I stood at the top of a rise and looked back over the tundra flats. The bearberry and dwarf birch lay crimson across the expanse, and behind us, Mt. Denali stood like a God even Renita could believe in. I don't know how to explain this feeling. I didn't even try to hide the tears from Renita, even when she shook her head, said "Jesus, men," and laughed.

THE LAST TIME I called Renita, I invited her to go out on the boat with me.

"Let's kayak," she said. "I like to be right down on the water."

So, I have planned a trip out of Valdez, mid-September, the weekend after Renita ends the llama trekking season. Three days, and we'll camp each night where we land. I imagine us together on the water. Renita, I know, will never love me. I'm glad that I love her. It is good to be loved, I think, good for her.

I can buy God as an artist who can never quite get us right. But maybe one day on the water, it will be just Renita and me and the waves and the kittiwakes and puffins and sea otters. Our slow gliding movements. Maybe just being together on a day which will surely be drizzly and blue and silver-gray, we will be of the light that surrounds us and somewhere the universe will stand back and admire, will feel the satisfaction that only comes during those rare moments when the art attempted has been achieved. And together on the water, our paddling strokes will synch, and I will try to frame it, an image to sustain me through the dark silence of impending winter.

ACKNOWLEDGMENTS

This collection owes greatly to the generosity and encouragement of more people than I can name, but I am especially grateful to:

Brent Spencer for his profound wisdom and patience in helping me put this book together and Jonis Agee for her on-going mentorship and unwavering faith in my work.

Erin Flanagan, for her friendship, feedback, generous insight and willingness to listen.

My creative writing colleagues at the University of Alaska Fairbanks, Stephen F. Austin State University, and the Fairbanks Summer Arts Festival: Sean Hill, Derick Burleson, Gerri Brightwell and Len Kamerling; John McDermott, Christine Butterworth-McDermott, Andrew Brininstool, Mark Sanders and Kimberly Verhines; and Jeanne Clark, Rob Davidson, Peggy Shumaker and Nicole Stellon O'Donnell.

The creative writing faculty at the University of Nebraska who gave many of these stories their earliest push: Judy Slater, Ted Kooser. And Gerry Shapiro, who is sorely missed.

My mentors from Breadloaf and the Taos and Nebraska Summer Writer's Conferences: Rick Bass, Luis Urrea (Cindy, too!), Greg Martin, Debra Earling and Jesse Lee Kercheval.

Erin Hollowell and Beth Kinsel for their willingness to read and provide feedback on specific stories.

Kelly Carlisle, Tyrone Jaeger, James Engelhardt and Jim Reese for providing a community, and making me feel we are all in this together.

Jim Perrizo, for always answering "Read any good books lately?" with a resounding "Yes." And for the conversations that follow that answer.

Curt Christensen, a storyteller if ever there was one. Wish I'd written it all down.

All former and current students from the BFA program at Stephen F. Austin State and the MFA program at the University of Alaska: please know that you inspire me daily. Keep writing!

My parents, Donald and Doris, and brother and sisters—David, Denise, Debbie and Deidra. You make me proud to be the 7th D. Thanks also to the in-laws: Lisa, Mike and Reed. And all the Essers and Trettins.

And finally, most importantly, Joan. For all that's happened since that day in Crowley when you knocked on that old schoolhouse door.

ABOUT THE AUTHOR

Daryl Farmer is the author of *Bicycling Beyond the Divide*, which received a Barnes and Noble Discover Great New Writers Award and was a Colorado Book Award finalist. Farmer's work has appeared in several journals including *Whitefish Review, Grist, Hayden's Ferry Review, South Dakota Review,* and *Quarter After Eight.* He received his M.A. and Ph.D. in creative writing from the University of Nebraska-Lincoln and has taught at Georgia Tech and Stephen F. Austin State University in Texas. Currently, he is an assistant professor and director of the MFA program at the University of Alaska-Fairbanks.